LESSER EVIL

CJ LYONS

Also By CJ Lyons:

Lucy Guardino Thrillers:
SNAKE SKIN
BLOOD STAINED
KILL ZONE
AFTER SHOCK
HARD FALL
BAD BREAK
LAST LIGHT
DEVIL SMOKE
OPEN GRAVE
GONE DARK

Renegade Justice Thrillers featuring Morgan Ames:
FIGHT DIRTY
RAW EDGES
ANGELS WEEP
LOOK AWAY
TRIP WIRE

Hart and Drake Medical Suspense:
NERVES OF STEEL
SLEIGHT OF HAND
FACE TO FACE
EYE OF THE STORM

Shadow Ops Covert Thrillers:
CHASING SHADOWS
LOST IN SHADOWS
EDGE OF SHADOWS

Fatal Insomnia Medical Thrillers:
FAREWELL TO DREAMS
A RAGING DAWN
THE SLEEPLESS STARS

Caitlyn Tierney FBI Thrillers:
BLIND FAITH
BLACK SHEEP
HOLLOW BONES

PRAISE FOR NEW YORK TIMES AND USA TODAY BESTSELLER CJ LYONS:

"Everything a great thriller should be—action packed, authentic, and intense." ~#1 *New York Times* bestselling author Lee Child

"A compelling new voice in thriller writing···I love how the characters come alive on every page." ~*New York Times* bestselling author Jeffery Deaver

"Top Pick! A fascinating and intense thriller." ~ 4 1/2 stars, *RT Book Reviews*

"An intense, emotional thriller···(that) climbs to the edge of intensity." ~*National Examiner*

"A perfect blend of romance and suspense. My kind of read." ~*#1 New York Times* Bestselling author Sandra Brown

"Highly engaging characters, heart-stopping scenes···one great rollercoaster ride that will not be stopping anytime soon." ~Bookreporter.com

"Adrenalin pumping." ~*The Mystery Gazette*

"Riveting." ~*Publishers Weekly Beyond Her Book*

Lyons "is a master within the genre." ~*Pittsburgh Magazine*

"Will leave you breathless and begging for more." ~Romance Novel TV

"A great fast-paced read···.Not to be missed." ~4 ½ Stars, Book Addict

"Breathtakingly fast-paced." ~*Publishers Weekly*

"Simply superb···riveting drama···a perfect ten." ~Romance Reviews Today

"Characters with beating hearts and three dimensions." ~*Newsday*

"A pulse-pounding adrenalin rush!" ~Lisa Gardner

"Packed with adrenalin." ~David Morrell

LESSER EVIL

CJ LYONS

"Those who choose the lesser evil forget quickly that they chose evil."
~Hannah Arendt

THE RUNNING GIRL WAS NAKED, bare feet pounding against the bridge's rough pavement, blood flying behind her with every stride.

It was two hours before dawn on a frigid October morning. Few drivers had reason to be heading over Pittsburgh's Hot Metal Bridge at this hour. One of the few, a truck driver, honked his horn, startled fully awake by the girl's sudden appearance. He did not stop. Later that day, as he continued his journey south through Maryland, Virginia, and finally North Carolina, he kept thinking about the girl. Was she real or a twist of his exhausted imagination? Why was she alone, naked on the bridge? And finally, who was she running from?

It wasn't until he stopped for the night and googled "naked girl bridge Pittsburgh" that he learned the truth and realized how very wrong he'd been.

The other three cars on the bridge braked and parked, blocking the road, their occupants watching as the girl stopped, hands on her knees, bent over, panting. Behind her, the lights of Pittsburgh's South Side shimmered against the black mirror of the Monongahela, making the bridge feel isolated, an island floating fifty feet above the water, surrounded by stars.

One driver, a sixty-three-year-old die cutter with daughters and granddaughters of his own, got out of his Buick and stepped toward her. "Miss? Are you all right? Let me help you."

The girl shook her head, her long hair whipping from side to side. She turned her face to him, eyes showing white, mouth curled into a feral snarl. "No. Get away. I have to do this."

He held his hands up in surrender but stood his ground. In the other lane, two more cars idled, although their occupants hadn't emerged. In the first, a twenty-something kid had rolled down his window to film the girl. His passenger, another kid, shouted something over the hip-hop beat that rocked their low-slung Camaro. It sounded like, "Do it, bitch!"

The final vehicle was a large, dark SUV with blacked-out windows, stopped far enough away that the grandfather couldn't make out any details, not make or year, not license plate number or state of origin. Later, he couldn't say for certain if it even had license plates at all. It idled, half hidden by the night. That's when he realized it had its headlights off—if it wasn't for the reflection of his own car's lights against the SUV's windshield, it would have been totally invisible. He wondered at that, felt a sudden rush of vulnerability standing out here exposed, no longer protected by his two tons of American steel.

A sense of movement made him whirl. The girl rushed toward the girders at the edge of the bridge, bloody footprints left in her wake as she climbed over one barrier, then hoisted herself up to the final steel beam, her body swaying. Now all that kept her from plunging into the river below was her shaky grip.

"Miss," he shouted, his words barely carrying over the wind sweeping through the steel and the kids' loud music. "Please, come down. Let me help."

The breeze caught her hair, billowing it like the ribbons his infant granddaughter loved to play with. This girl looked nothing like any of his girls, not with her wild eyes and neck corded tight with anguished muscles. And yet... He risked a step toward her, not that he could ever reach her in time, not if she decided to let go. Holding her gaze with his, not looking where he was going, he stretched out a hand, palm up. "Please, miss. Whatever it is, it's not worth it."

She jerked her chin up at that, defiant. Her gaze swiveled past him to the Camaro and then the SUV. "You're wrong. He is."

Before he could say anything, she released her grip, spun around, spread her arms like wings, and flew.

Chapter 1

Four days later...

Dr. Cassandra Hart placed her palm on the dead girl's forehead, a silent benediction. The skin was cold, colder than she'd expected—although she should have anticipated it; the morgue attendant had moments ago wheeled the plastic-shrouded body from the refrigerated storage room. Maybe it was because as an ER physician Cassie's experience with death came in the form of patients passing before her eyes, beneath her helping hands striving to pump life back into their still-warm bodies. Unlike here in the morgue, no one in the ER was ever cold and dead.

Alina Dolya had been only nineteen when she leaped to her death from the Hot Metal Bridge, leaving no family behind to claim her body. Ensuring that she wasn't cremated and entombed forever in an anonymous cardboard box was the least Cassie could do for the girl. After all, it was Cassie's fault that she was dead.

Not that Cassie's name appeared anywhere in

the pages of the autopsy; she was there only as a courtesy, an observer. The ME had listed the cause of death as drowning; the manner: suicide.

Nowhere in his report of Alina's physical characteristics did he mention the way her one eyebrow rose whenever she'd smiled, how she'd lisped slightly when she'd tried to pronounce unfamiliar English words, or how her hands had trembled until she'd clench them so tight her fingernails would leave deeply grooved crescents in her palms whenever she'd told her story. Not the story of her life; the story of her first death, which had happened when Cassie had met her in the ER, brought in as a Jane Doe, suffering hypothermia so severe the medics had called her in as a "popsicle."

That was nine months ago. Cassie had brought Alina back to life, warming her inside and out. But then had come the real work: examining the injuries that had led to Alina being dumped naked in an alley on a moonless January night. Injuries listed now as "incidental findings" in the autopsy report, scars healed but never forgotten—not by Alina in life, not by Cassie now that Alina was dead.

It didn't matter how the coroner labeled Alina's death. In her heart, Cassie knew that Alina hadn't taken her own life; Alina's life had been stolen. By a monster who still walked free, hunting for his next victim.

Cassie nodded her thanks to the assistant, signed the paperwork he presented her, and then retraced her steps through the medical examiner's complex. Its too-bright, too-cheerful decor felt as forced as a hothouse geranium, jarring and unnatural. Or maybe it was her own mood. Unlike the people who worked here, speaking for the dead while serving the living, she felt each patient she lost as a betrayal. This time a failure not of her medical skills, but rather of the justice system. She, the police, the courts—they had all failed Alina.

But Cassie had failed Alina first. Now it was up to Cassie to try to redeem herself. Not only because it was Cassie's fault Alina had died, but because there was no one else to fight Alina's battle.

Cassie reached the parking lot. The October morning sunshine felt less bright than the artificial lights inside the building. Still, it was a relief to inhale fully without the scent of Ozium and other chemicals polluting each breath. Her husband, Detective Mickey Drake, leaned against the side of his classic Mustang, a vehicle immensely impractical for Pittsburgh winters but that he refused to part with. He was watching her, assessing her posture, her gait, her expression. Drake was like that. In an instant, he could devour every detail of a crime scene—or translate Cassie's every nuance.

He pushed away from the car, sliding his phone into his pocket, and met her halfway. Without a word, he wrapped his arms around her. They stood there for several moments, oblivious to the ambulances and hearses pulling up to the building behind them, not caring that anyone saw, simply steadying each other with a shared strength.

"Our first kiss was in this morgue," he said.

As they walked to the car, her hand slid down to capture his in a movement that was automatic, as natural as breathing. "That kiss almost got you fired."

His fingers tightened around hers. "Almost got you killed."

"Did you reach your FBI friend?"

"Former FBI," he corrected. "Lucy's testifying for the feds this morning. I spoke with her boss at Beacon Falls, Valencia Frazier."

"I'm still not sure about this Beacon Falls group. Maybe—"

"They're good," he assured her. "Think NCMEC but for adults." He pronounced the acronym for the National Center for Missing and Exploited Children as nick-mick. "A nonprofit, none of the red tape of official channels."

"But you said they specialize in missing persons and cold cases. Alina isn't missing—" Not anymore. The image of the plastic-sheeted cocoon the morgue assistant had trundled away haunted Cassie. So cold, anonymous. Was she the only one who would remember Alina as a person?

"Much as I hate to admit it, you're at a dead end with us." He meant the Pittsburgh Police Bureau, where Drake worked on the Major Crimes Squad. "And you've gotten nowhere with the feds. The PPB already has a consulting contract with the Beacon Group."

"But Detective Carter—she's worked so hard." Stephanie Carter was the sex crimes detective assigned to Alina's case. She was young, but Cassie couldn't fault her work. Stefi had followed every lead. The problem was, with so little evidence, every lead led to nowhere.

"She's totally fine with asking for a second opinion, fresh eyes." His gaze rested on her, and she knew exactly what his unspoken question was: Why was Cassie suddenly balking?

She lowered her face, studied the cracked macadam of the parking lot. He lay a hand at the small of her back as if bracing her. "I don't want to fail her. Not again. I can't."

He wrapped his arms around her. "You won't," he whispered.

After a long moment, they parted. "When?"

He opened her car door for her. "Today. Eleven. But it doesn't mean they'll take the case. Just that they'll listen." Once she was settled into her seat, he crossed around to the driver's side, took his time adjusting his seat belt, saying nothing for a long moment.

"Could the ME tell when—" Drake's question drifted into silence.

"Several days before she died, best he could tell."

He jerked his chin in a reluctant nod. "Jimmy said they're taking one last run with the cadaver dogs, but with the river—"

Cassie shuddered. What had happened to Alina was even worse than Drake knew, but soon she'd have to tell the story to the people at Beacon Falls. It was a story she had the strength to tell only once, so she kept her silence.

Drake started the car, the throaty grumble of its engine vibrating through the floorboards. He steered them out of the parking lot, and they headed east on Penn Avenue. She closed her eyes and leaned her head against her window. A disapproving silence wafted from his direction. She didn't need to see the frown that tugged his eyebrows together to know why. It was an argument he'd already lost several times.

"This actor—" he started, then stopped. He tried again. "This case. You know we did everything we could." Cassie knew he meant "we" as in the entire police department. Drake didn't investigate sexual assaults; his purview was homicide. "You need to know this is a long shot. I'm not sure what Lucy and her team might be able to do that we couldn't."

She knew he was torn between his desire to protect her from the pain of failure and her need to see justice done. "I know. But I need to try. I owe Alina that."

"You don't owe Alina anything—" That earned him a glare. Her patients were no less important than the victims he worked with at Major Crimes. He backtracked. "I mean, you've already gone above and beyond. Without you, we would not even have known—"

"Maybe without me pushing so hard..." Alina wouldn't be dead, she finished the thought. "I should have trusted you."

"You think this is your fault? No. Never." He

reached his hand past the gearshift to squeeze her arm. "Hart. What you did—what you're doing—no one could have done more. Just promise me."

She braced herself. She knew what was coming, had heard it too many times before. "If your FBI friend says she can't help, this is the end of it." She recited the words in a monotone. "If she can't figure out a way, then I'll give up. Quit."

They were the words he wanted to hear, but somehow, she knew she hadn't convinced him. Probably because she wasn't convinced herself.

But Drake surprised her. "Actually, what I was going to say was, promise me you'll let Lucy and her team work the case. You're only there to answer medical questions. And once they take the case, you can do that by phone." Traffic slowed for a red light, and he turned to focus on her. "Promise me. You won't do anything dangerous. You won't do anything that you even think might be dangerous. This guy—"

He shook his head, the car lurching slightly as traffic surged forward and he mistimed his shift into second. Which told her everything about how upset he really was. "I don't want you anywhere near this guy. Hell, I don't even want you on the same planet as this actor." Despite the traffic, now moving briskly, he turned to look at her. "Promise me."

Cassie rested her hand on top of his on the gearshift. "I promise. I won't do anything dangerous."

He nodded and released a sigh. And she knew he wanted nothing more than to turn the car around and drive to Mexico if that was what it would take to keep her safe. Instead, he gripped the wheel tighter, hunched his shoulders, and hit the gas. Because that's not who they were. They didn't run away from danger. They ran toward it.

It was why he'd fallen in love with her and she him. But every time Cassie thought of Alina, of what she'd endured, the depravity, the callous disregard for human life, she felt more than anger at the injustice. She felt fear. Cold as the deepest ocean on the darkest night, flooding over her, drowning her.

So far, she'd managed to hide it from Drake—or he was hiding the fact that he knew how scared she was, she wasn't sure. Because her fear made no difference. They had to stop this... this—she couldn't bring herself to think of him as a man; the things he'd done had proven him less than human—this beast.

There was no one left to do it, to put an end to the terror. No one except for Cassie. And Drake's FBI friend, Lucy Guardino.

Chapter 2

During her fifteen years as an FBI agent, Lucy Guardino had never enjoyed testifying. Not even here in front of the federal grand jury where it was only her and an assistant US attorney sharing their side of the story in an effort to persuade twenty-three civilians to allow them to charge a criminal and proceed with a trial.

Lucy shifted in her wooden chair, trying not to appear as if she was uncomfortable or nervous. Unlike in a regular courtroom, here there was no witness box, no physical barriers between her and the people watching and judging. Despite the dark wood paneling, maroon carpet, and ornate plaster wreaths and decorations covering the ceiling, the grand jury room was designed to evoke a feeling of equality. No judge sitting on high, no defense attorney performing for his client—no defendant present at all, in fact. It was an intimate stage, suitable for the unraveling of secrets and conspiracies.

A stage with a very specific audience—which was

why Lucy hated testifying. Somehow, speaking the truth here, the truth as shaped by an AUSA's questions and commentary, felt more like a performance and less like justice, despite the oaths all involved swore.

Lucy decided to cross her legs—the most comfortable and engaging posture the rigid wooden chair would allow. As she waited for Graham Hunt to begin his questioning, she made eye contact with each juror, sharing a quiet smile. It was early in the day, so they were still alert, interested, which boded well. She was surprised that Hunt had decided to prosecute the case himself—he'd been an AUSA three years ago when the case broke, but it'd taken that long for charges to wind their way through the federal system. In the meantime, the new administration had appointed Graham Hunt US attorney for Western Pennsylvania, an honor that usually meant the start of a political career and an end to courtroom appearances.

Lucy had hoped that after leaving the FBI six months ago she would never need to see the inside of a courtroom again. But this case... She understood why Hunt couldn't let it go. This case still haunted her, not only the crimes and the men behind them, but also the consequences. Because she hadn't been able to save all of the victims, not this time.

She smoothed the crease in her navy slacks, forcing the dark memories aside as she assumed the neutral mask of a professional, burying her personal and very unprofessional feelings. Hunt finished introducing her to the jury, presenting her various qualifications in a conversational manner as if he were one of the jurors and not the director of this peculiar production. Finally, he turned to Lucy, flashing her a smile only she could see, before removing his Italian designer suit jacket and carefully rolling up his shirt sleeves. His every movement was choreographed to proclaim that he wasn't some rich politician—although he was, as the Hunt name equaled both money and power—but rather a man of the people, right there beside them, down in the trenches, fighting for truth and justice.

He turned his back on the jurors to face Lucy and threw her a wink, suddenly appearing younger than his forty-three years. "Former Supervisory Special Agent Guardino, could you please tell us of your involvement in Operation Three Rivers?"

Hunt settled in, leaning casually against the wall closest to the jurors so when Lucy addressed him, she also addressed the twenty-three civilians eager to finally learn which case had summoned them here this morning. The fact that they were a "special" grand jury meant the case had to do with organized crime or government corruption—in this case, both. Hunt had kept the names of the accused secret—not even Lucy knew all of the people under investigation. She was merely here to share her small part of what Hunt promised her was a very large criminal conspiracy.

She cleared her throat and answered his question. "Our investigation began three years ago when one of our cyberanalysts alerted the FBI to a major sex-trade operation centered here in Pittsburgh."

"You're kidding. Human trafficking here? C'mon, this is Pittsburgh." He ignored Lucy to glance at the people alongside him, using his voice as their voice. As if he wasn't a prosecutor trying to bend the jury to his will, but rather part of a group of friends debating current events. One thing about Hunt, he knew how to play the game and play it well. Given their targets—some of them men considered above reproach, names the jury would recognize, Hunt had told her—he had to be at the top of his game today if justice was to be served. And so did Lucy. She straightened her posture, kept her tone professional while slowing her words so the jury would miss nothing.

"We verified the information, working with DEA, ICE, and Interpol. We traced drugs manufactured in the Netherlands to Marseilles, where some of it was used to purchase women from Belarus and the Ukraine, along with female refugees from Syria. The remaining drugs and the women were then shipped to the port of Savannah—the women enduring inhumane conditions in the holds of cargo ships, often suffering multiple sexual assaults by the crew. Once they reached the United States, the Zapata cartel took over, distributing the drugs along the Eastern Seaboard while the women were transported here to Pittsburgh. As head of the Western Pennsylvania Sexual Assault Felony Enforcement squad for the FBI, it was my team's job to lead the local investigation, apprehend the suspects involved, and rescue the trafficked women."

"That sounds horrible. How come we didn't ever hear anything about this?" His tone held a hint of incredulity, mirroring the attitudes of his jurors. "Why didn't the FBI and DEA make this public? It would have been a major media event."

"The DEA had undercover agents infiltrating the drug ring, and they needed to be protected." Lucy didn't mention the multiple corrupt police officers and other officials who were involved—it was up to Hunt to build the case against each of them, which meant a slow and gradual process. He'd instructed Lucy to focus on the human element of the case, wanting the jury emotionally involved before he turned to a dry recitation of the money trail. "My own focus was on rescuing the victims as soon as possible, before they were moved to another location or trafficked further."

"Trafficked further?"

Lucy shifted her gaze from Hunt to the jury, making sure they understood. "It's not an uncommon practice for traffickers to sell off the women they hold prisoner, to make room for fresh victims that their customers will pay a premium to exploit."

"And by exploit, you mean—"

"Rape." She let the ugly word hang in the air. "Sexually assault by forcing them to perform on-camera and off-camera sex acts to put money in the pockets of the traffickers and to gratify men willing to pay to treat women as disposable objects."

"So, we're not talking prostitutes walking the

streets, able to ask for help if they wanted."

As if those women weren't also prisoners to their circumstances. But this wasn't the time or place to debate the realities of the sex trade. She shifted in her seat, addressing the jury. "No. These women were held captive, kept in a warehouse not two blocks away from Pittsburgh Police Bureau Headquarters on the North Side. They never left the building. Some had not seen the sun in months. In addition to the occasional carefully vetted in-person customer, they were being used for Internet porn. The highest bidder could script whatever he wanted done to them and view it on his computer in the comfort of his own home."

Hunt made a noise low in his throat. He ran a hand through his hair, a seemingly casual gesture that made him look like a young Robert Redford, then turned to the jurors, obviously upset. "We're going to show you a few select photos now. I warn you, they are disturbing. However, it is our duty to bear witness—it is the only way to honor these victims."

He reached for a remote, then turned off the lights. The first image, a young woman, obviously terrified, was shown from the shoulders up, hanging from her chained arms. Tears streamed through her heavy makeup, and blood dripped from her lip. More than one of the jurors gasped, despite the fact that the image was no more graphic than any PG-13 horror film.

"Ms. Guardino, these images are indicative of what these women endured?" Hunt asked as he clicked through the photos, going just fast enough for the jury to appreciate the horrors without giving them too much time to dwell on details. Smart. They needed empathy from the jury, not revulsion.

"Yes. We captured much more graphic images on servers we seized at the facility, including several videos of women being tortured and gang-raped." Lucy had to fight to keep the emotion from her voice.

She'd interviewed the man who'd owned the building and been a frequent patron, appearing on the tapes, always selecting the youngest, most frightened girl. A former state representative turned lobbyist, he'd been narcissistic enough to actually take pride in the multinational, multimillion-dollar business he'd helped to create. Couched in terms of a hypothetical, he'd offered Lucy a lesson on successful business practices.

"We go where the profit is," he'd told Lucy after she'd shown him some of the more horrific images in a vain attempt at finding some sliver of remorse in the man who'd campaigned on a "family values" platform and was a grandfather of girls the same age as his victims. "Exactly like any successful business. We give the customer what they want. Blame the customers— we're just fulfilling a need. You wouldn't arrest Hershey's for causing tooth rot or obesity or diabetes. You don't see them as evil. We're no different."

As the images flicked past, Lucy's hands curled into fists, hidden by the shadows. Finally, Hunt turned off the projector, leaving the room in a sudden intimate darkness. Not unlike what the victims might have suffered during their captivity, Lucy noted. Hunt reached for the lights, prolonging the moment before flicking them on and facing the jury, his shoulders slumped because of what they'd all just witnessed together. Then he sighed heavily. "Tell me. Who are these men? How did they get away with this...this horror, here in the heart of Pittsburgh?"

"Off-duty Pittsburgh police officers guarded the production studio and the women, and we discovered that several prominent police and county administrators were involved." The higher the rank, the quicker they'd made plea bargains, rolling on their underlings but never the men pulling the strings. Another reason why it'd taken three long years to build a case. "But the real leaders, the ones who pocketed the profit—"

Hunt motioned her to silence as the door opened, and a man hurried in, handing Hunt a note and whispering in his ear. The man was average height, wearing a conservative suit typical of the lawyers who frequented the courthouse, but his bearing spoke of a military or law enforcement background. His gaze circled the room, dissecting possible threats, his hands never dropping below his waist, where, in any other setting, Lucy was certain he'd have a weapon holstered. She knew all this because it was exactly the same way she entered a room.

The jurors leaned forward, excited by the drama as Hunt unfolded the paper and read it in silence. He glanced at Lucy, his eyes narrowed, before resuming a neutral expression and turning to the jurors. "Ladies and gentlemen, I'm afraid we'll need to recess for the day, as an urgent matter requires my presence elsewhere. We'll reconvene here Monday at nine. Thank you for your time. Enjoy your long weekend."

The jurors murmured among themselves as they gathered their belongings and filed out, leaving only Lucy, Hunt, and the man.

"What the hell was that?" she demanded as soon as the door closed behind the last juror. "Why'd you stop? An urgent matter, needed elsewhere—makes it seem like this case isn't so important after all."

He didn't answer her, his hands deep in the pockets of his slacks as he scrutinized the blank plaster wall behind Lucy, the wall he'd used as a projector screen. Lucy turned to the man who'd brought the note. "Lucy Guardino," she introduced herself when he remained silent.

"Jared Estanza." He announced his name—no rank, no organizational affiliation—as if it were classified information.

Hunt glanced at them both. "Relax, Jared. She's one of the good guys." He turned to Lucy. "Jared's with Homeland Security Investigations. Office of the Inspector General."

Lucy raised her eyebrow at that. The Inspector General functioned like the FBI's Office of Professional Responsibility or a police department's Internal Affairs Division, empowered with investigating wrongdoing in their own ranks. Which meant Hunt and Estanza were investigating federal agents.

Hunt reread the note. He paced the area in front of the blank wall. Without turning back to Lucy, he asked, "You ever testify in one of the original courtrooms? The ones with the murals that FDR commissioned?"

"Yeah, they were part of the CCC." Like most of the parks and roads and other public works around Pittsburgh. "What does that note say?"

"You know, there was once another painting." He reached his fingers to stroke the empty wall. "It was called Modern Justice. Hung right here, in fact. Massive piece, took up the entire wall. Until it fell down during a trial. After that, it was lost forever."

He returned to Lucy, handing her the paper. "They say it depicted Lady Justice as both a protector of the innocent and an avenging angel against the guilty. I kinda wish it was still here to remind folks why we do what we do."

As he spoke, Lucy skimmed the note. It was a police report. A man had been killed that morning, hit by a car. Then she saw the victim's name. The accountant who'd tied the day-to-day operations of the trafficking ring to the men who'd profited from it. Their main witness, due to appear later today.

"Any chance it wasn't an accident?" she asked.

"No," Estanza answered. "From the witness statements, just wrong time, wrong place."

"Seriously?" Lucy allowed her incredulity to color her tone. Estanza shot her a glare, then focused on Hunt, an eyebrow raised, obviously questioning Lucy's right to challenge him.

Hunt didn't intervene, instead glanced at the door as if wishing Lucy would leave. That's when it hit her. She was truly now on the outside, no longer trusted with any information other than what the regular public would be given.

She turned to Hunt. "We can still nail them. You've got my testimony and Taylor's." Taylor was the FBI analyst who'd initially discovered the trafficking ring. "Plus, the co-conspirators who rolled, and we obtained U visas for two of the victims—" She'd hoped Fatima and Maria wouldn't need to testify until the trial, but...

"No." Hunt glanced at Estanza.

"ICE rescinded their visas," Estanza told her. "Deported both of them."

ICE? Maybe that was why Estanza was here, Immigration and Customs agents would fall under his purview. "So we track them down, bring them back."

"We tried," Hunt answered. "They're gone, in the wind."

"Maybe one of the other victims—"

"They've all returned to their home countries, and none of them are cooperating," Estanza cut her off. Even his poker face couldn't mask his frustration.

Hunt blew out his breath, shoulders slumping. "It's done. Without firsthand victim testimony and the money trail the accountant would have given us, we'll never win at trial. Not against him."

Him. The anonymous target of the special grand jury. The man Hunt once told her would be more difficult to prosecute than Santa Claus, he was that well known and popular. Lucy had no idea who this leader of a conspiracy that spanned three continents was, but it was obvious Hunt had turned his quest for justice into something extremely personal. "We can't just—"

"Lucy," he snapped. He raised both hands, palms toward her as if surrendering. "It's done. Thanks for all your hard work. But it's over. We've gone as far as we can. I'm sorry."

He spun on his heel and walked out the door, Estanza following him, leaving Lucy staring at the large blank wall in a room where Justice once resided.

CHAPTER 3

AFTER LUCY LEFT THE COURTHOUSE and reached her Subaru parked in the public lot two blocks away, she was still too angry to drive. Fatima and Maria deserved justice, just as the other women did. How could Hunt give up so easily?

She didn't even unlock the car. Instead, she paced the lot, ignoring the curious stare of the attendant in his booth. She read and reread the police report, scrutinizing it for clues to something more nefarious than a simple traffic accident and finding none. The victim had been crossing against the light. Witnesses said he'd darted into the street right into the path of the driver, a librarian at the Carnegie late for a doctor's appointment, who had been making a left turn, pushing an amber light, but doing nothing illegal.

Still... Lucy hated coincidences, and the timing couldn't have been worse. She slid her phone from her pocket and called Taylor, one of her former team members at the FBI. He'd helped break the case originally. She explained about their witness' untimely death. "Not sure if Hunt's even going to reconvene the grand jury. You might not need to testify."

"Testify? I was never subpoenaed."

"What?" She finished another lap, returning to her Subaru, this time getting into the car. "I'm sure he expected you—"

"Maybe he was afraid going through official channels might leak?" Taylor was fond of conspiracy theories—and unfortunately, he often was right to be suspicious. "Last thing he'd want is for his targets to know they were the subject of a grand jury, right? It'd give them time to try to shut him down."

"Time? They've already had more than enough time—" She started the car but didn't put it into drive. "We should have moved faster." But the previous US attorney had insisted on turning Lucy's case over to a special multijurisdictional, multiagency task force. Three years really wasn't that long to develop such a large RICO case, but clearly Lucy's victims were considered expendable if their part of the case became untenable.

"We did the best we could." Taylor sounded distracted, no doubt multitasking even as they spoke. Lucy had a sudden pang of regret—as much as she loved her new team at Beacon Falls, she missed Taylor and Walden and the rest of her FBI family.

"Could you do me a favor? Go through the case files one last time, see if there's any new evidence you could give Hunt to act on." Since Lucy was no longer

FBI, she didn't have access to restricted evidence.

"Sure, I'll try. Take care." He hung up, leaving Lucy alone with her frustrations. She was surprised Taylor wasn't more upset—it had been his first big case—but now that he was working white-collar crimes, he had plenty of new cases to divide his attention. Just like, according to a reminder text from her boss, Valencia Frazier, she had a new case of her own at Beacon Falls. She sighed and steered toward the parking lot exit, ready to pay for her morning spent seeking justice.

By the time she arrived at the centuries-old Beacon Falls mansion, home to generations of Fraziers, she was debating a call to one of her police contacts, despite the fact that she had no authority to request information. Another perk she'd lost when she left the FBI. Hunt or Estanza would follow up, she told herself. They could ask the questions she couldn't. In fact, maybe they already were pursuing other angles to use before the grand jury—they just didn't want Lucy to be involved, now that she was no longer with the Bureau.

She wasn't sure if the thought made her feel angry or insulted. After all, it wasn't as if her investigative abilities had diminished simply because of her ankle injury—which was finally healing properly. Besides, the FBI had forced her to accept a medical retirement because of internal politics; her injury was merely a convenient excuse.

Still, the urge to do something, anything, to save the case nagged her even as she passed through the estate's gates and parked her car. Lost in her thoughts of various strategies she could present to Hunt to resurrect their case, Lucy barely noticed the receptionist's wave as she passed through the hand-carved oak doors and climbed the stairs to her team's office.

She took her customary seat at the middle of the elegant Queen Anne dining table that served as her team's work area and tried to clear her mind before her next meeting. At least, by not finishing her testimony, she wasn't running late.

The Beacon Falls estate had been in Valencia Frazier's family for over two hundred years, and she'd maintained as much of the history as possible. The room Lucy's team worked out of was graced with hand-painted wallpaper, beautiful carved mahogany bookcases that reached from floor to ceiling, and paintings depicting the original Frazier trading post where both settlers and Native Americans had prospered. Compared to Lucy's old office at the FBI, with its glass walls and utilitarian furnishings, somedays it felt surreal to come to work here at Beacon Falls. In many ways, she was still doing the same job—finding missing persons, tracking predators—but the crimes the Beacon Group handled were ones regular law enforcement had gotten nowhere with, cases long gone cold as dust.

Wash, the youngest member of Lucy's team and their resident tech genius, rolled through the door. He parked his wheelchair at the head of the table, monitors to both sides, keyboard in front of him. Now that Beacon Falls had added forensic genealogy to its repertoire, Wash was busier than ever assisting the police with cold cases and helping NamUs identify previously unidentified murder victims. Despite the extra hours, he bounced his chair off its wheels with his usual irrepressible energy. "How come TK lives so close it's a five-minute walk up the drive, but she's the one who's always late? I thought they teach punctuality in the Marines."

"What they teach is fifty ways to kill a man with your bare hands," TK quipped, walking through the door carrying a silver tray brimming with pastries. She arched an eyebrow in Wash's direction as she set the tray on the table in front of the empty chairs reserved for their guests. "Valencia waylaid me. Guess this Hart chick must have impressed her."

"Her story did," Lucy said. "It was her husband, Mickey Drake, Valencia spoke with—he's a detective, Major Crimes Squad, Pittsburgh Police Bureau."

"You work with him before?" Wash asked, reaching for the tray only to have TK bat his hand away and slide it farther down the table, parking it in front of the chair where she sprawled. In contrast to her runway-model good looks, TK wore desert camo combat boots, torn jeans, and a ragged Cabela's tee. Lucy often wondered what drove the younger woman's attempts at camouflage, as if poor posture and shabby clothes could ever allow TK to hide in plain sight.

"No, but my old team at the FBI vouched for him," Lucy answered Wash. "Said he's boots-on-the-ground kind of police." She aimed this at TK, knowing the former Marine MP didn't always get along with bureaucrats or desk jockeys. "He's got a good closure rate, was the guy who caught that serial killer targeting school kids."

"I thought his name was familiar," Wash said. "And his wife's a doctor? Think she'd be interested in taking over for Tommy?"

Tommy Worth, their medical consultant, had moved out of the area, leaving Lucy's team short-handed. She and TK did the field work, Wash handled the databases and other technical evidence review, but without Tommy they were at the mercy of the forensic experts Valencia persuaded to donate consultation time. It helped that the Beacon Group was a nonprofit with a stellar reputation, but in her short time here, Lucy had come to realize that their real secret weapon was Valencia's wit and charm. Valencia had founded the Beacon Group in the hopes of finding answers to her husband's unsolved disappearance. Despite her own tragedy, she never faltered in her mission to help other families suffering the same fate.

"Doubt it. Dr. Hart works part time at the ER over at Three Rivers and runs a free clinic in East Liberty." Lucy didn't mention it, but Cassandra Hart had been one of the ER doctors who'd saved her life after a hit man had targeted her and her family back in January.

A knock came at the door. Lucy walked over and answered it. A dark-haired woman with a flawless olive-skinned complexion stood waiting, her hands cradling a document box. Behind her stood a tall man with equally dark hair and riveting blue eyes.

"Lucy Guardino?" the woman asked as Lucy took the box from her and set it on the table. "I'm Cassandra Hart. This is my husband, Detective Mickey Drake."

Hart moved with fluid precision, taking a seat at the table near the box, then sliding it closer to her. Drake paused, assessing the room with the practiced eyes of a law enforcement professional before following his wife. He nodded to Lucy. "Nice to finally meet. Your guys, Taylor and Walden, were a huge help last December."

"So I heard." Lucy had been in Virginia, visiting her husband's parents, when Drake had called for the FBI's help after Hart had been kidnapped. "Glad you're both okay."

Hart made a waving motion with her hand, dismissing the incident despite the worry lines that appeared on her husband's face. He didn't want to be here, didn't like her getting involved with this case, Lucy surmised, watching as he placed one hand over Hart's arm, his body angled toward the door, ready to pull her out if need be.

Lucy made introductions. "This is George Washington Gamble, our tech analyst."

"Call me Wash, Dr. Hart. Or, if you prefer, resident god of technology." Wash circled his hand in a flourish, making everyone smile. Despite his youth—he'd only just turned twenty-two—he had a way of placing people at ease. Lucy often wondered if that skill had come before or after he'd been shot during a drive-by, ending up in a wheelchair when he was twelve years old.

"It's Cassie," Hart answered. "Please."

"And this is TK O'Connor, former Marine MP. She's our field investigator," Lucy finished, resuming her seat. She noted the way TK and Drake assessed each other—two alphas sniffing the air—and smiled. Lucy's husband, Nick, a psychologist who worked with law enforcement and the military, would appreciate the moment.

"I don't get it." TK broke the silence, her blond curls bouncing as she leaned forward in her chair. "I reviewed what Carter, the sex crimes detective, sent over. Alina Dolya committed suicide—we all saw the video those asswipes shot of her jumping off the Hot Metal Bridge. Here at Beacon Falls, we specialize in cold cases and missing persons. Not suicides or sexual assaults. What exactly do you want us to investigate?"

Lucy winced. TK was not known for her subtlety. From the pained look on Cassandra Hart's face, this case hit very close to home for the physician.

"We do want you to investigate a missing person," Hart said, avoiding TK's eyes to meet Lucy's gaze. "One that the police have already written off as dead." Drake flinched at that, but otherwise his expression did not change. "One that nobody is looking for, except for us."

"Who?" TK asked, a challenge more than a question.

"I just came from Alina's autopsy. They

confirmed it. She gave birth shortly before she killed herself. Her baby is missing."

CHAPTER 4

"Tʜᴇʀᴇ ᴡᴀs ɴᴏ ʙᴀʙʏ ɪɴ ᴛʜᴇ ᴠɪᴅᴇᴏ," TK, the former Marine, said before Cassie could begin to explain her theory. No. More than a theory. Her hope. Alina's baby had to be alive.

"The police couldn't find any trace of it, think Alina killed it," Drake answered. "Disposed of the body but was overwhelmed with guilt and then committed suicide." He nodded at Cassie. "They wouldn't have known Alina was pregnant if it hadn't been for Hart. She got them to start looking for the baby before the ME even did the autopsy."

"Why don't you start at the beginning?" Lucy suggested. "Tell us everything."

Cassie closed her eyes for a brief moment, remembering that dreary January day when she first met Alina. She felt Drake shift in his seat beside her, anticipating their audience's reaction.

"Nine months ago, the medics brought in a hypothermic victim, a young woman found naked, dumped in an alley in East Liberty. No vitals on the scene, but my team, we brought her back." Cassie had to work to keep her tone clinical.

"And that was Alina?" Wash asked.

"Yes." She paused for a moment, deciding against detailing the intimate details of Alina's assault. These were law enforcement professionals; they wouldn't be persuaded to take the case based on Alina's pain and suffering. They were looking for new leads to pursue, beyond what the police had already covered. "I did a rape kit, documented everything, called the police. Once Alina was stabilized, we interviewed her, but her memory was fragmented. She had difficulty piecing the events together, couldn't remember most of the actual assault."

"Was that because of the hypothermia?" Lucy asked. "Or something else?"

"Alina's tox screen was positive for metabolites of GHB and Rohypnol—both of which cause amnesia."

"Date-rape drugs," Lucy said.

"Exactly. Only this combo is a new synthetic formulation. The lab says they've never seen it before."

"Forensics?" TK asked. "You did a full rape kit, right?"

"Her attacker had bathed her with bleach, scrubbed her raw. We found no DNA, no hairs, nothing beyond finger marks on her skin where he choked her and held her down."

"Prints? With an alternative light source..." the kid, Wash, interjected, his tone eager.

Cassie shook her head. "We tried. Nothing. Alina

was held by her captor for several days. They'd already faded."

"So," TK said, edging her chair into the table and leaning forward, "you have no forensics and a victim whose memory was conveniently erased by drugs." She narrowed her gaze. "Those drugs are also popular with the rave and club crowd. Are we sure Alina didn't take them herself? Maybe the sex was consensual—or started that way?"

"I don't think nearly dying naked in an alley was consensual," Lucy snapped.

TK didn't back down. "I'm just saying—" She gestured with both hands as if frustrated already by Alina's case. "The police file focused on the rapist being a stranger. If she took the drugs consensually, maybe they should be looking closer to home—for the rapist and the baby. After all, if you're going to kill yourself, usually that starts with problems with the people you're close to, not total strangers."

"Alina was here from the Ukraine on a work visa. She rented a room from a retired nurse who said she never had visitors, never went out on dates or had late nights, and there were no signs of drug use," Cassie answered.

"Still, with no forensics—" TK persisted.

Cassie met the other woman's eyes, but it was Drake who took up the implied challenge. He slid the document box away from Cassie and opened it, then stood and walked around the table, distributing folders with the copies of the photos documenting Alina's injuries, slapping them down like playing cards.

"We do have forensics," Cassie said after giving them a few minutes to look at what Alina had endured—and hopefully connect with her as a person. "As part of the rape kit, we did a routine pregnancy test. It was positive."

"It was the rapist's baby Alina gave birth to?" TK made a small scoffing sound. Cassie waited until the younger woman met her gaze. TK's expression wasn't merely the cynicism of someone who knew the challenge that lay before them. As TK knotted one hand through her hair, Cassie realized the woman was angry—and in pain. This case hit too close to home. "And then she killed herself?"

"You think the baby is alive," Lucy said.

"Yes," Cassie answered. "We can find him—the baby. With your help."

"Wait," TK said, placing her palms on the file folder, holding it shut. As if not seeing Alina's face would give her some distance from the pain Alina had endured. "If it's a boy, it has a Y chromosome that comes from the father, right?"

"Yes," Cassie said. "After Alina decided to keep the baby, we hoped to use the baby's DNA to help find her attacker. There are new methods of determining paternity through the mother's blood."

"Right," Wash said. "Because mothers carry some cells from their babies with them the rest of their life."

"Exactly. And during pregnancy, mothers have a significant percentage of those fetal cells, enough that we can sample their DNA, then compare them to the father's."

Now it was Lucy who appeared skeptical—and she had every right to. "But that's comparing against a known DNA source, a simple paternity test. What you're suggesting is building a DNA profile against an unknown source. I'm no physician, but I'm pretty sure there's far too many variables to simply strip away what comes from the mother and declare the rest to be paternal origin."

"No, you're right. We—" Cassie's voice caught. "I thought it would at least give the police something to go on. Create a John Doe DNA profile based solely on the baby's Y chromosome to run against CODIS and the other DNA databases. If the rapist—or one of his male relatives—is in the system, they'd be a step ahead. Maybe save the next victim before he got to her."

"But you and the police needed the DA to sign off on a John Doe warrant—"

"And they'd have to go to the judge. Since it's based on new science—"

"The DA wanted you to explain it," Lucy said.

Cassie nodded. "And they wanted to meet Alina. See what kind of witness she'd make, how bad her memory loss was. Because once they got to court, it'd still come down to her."

"Okay," TK said, her posture relaxing a bit. "What went wrong?"

"That was three months ago. July. I was waiting on the courthouse steps for Alina, to take her in to meet the DA. I saw her across the street. She waved to me. Then a black SUV drove up, no markings. Two men got out. The one closest to me wore an ICE windbreaker. I heard Alina shout, and I ran. But they drove off just as I got there. They took her."

"Immigration? Why?" TK asked.

"Alina was here working as a model for an advertising agency. She had a visa, but after her pregnancy became obvious her boss fired her, canceled her visa. But the DA said he would get her a new one." She didn't tell them about how excited Alina had been when she'd learned that staying in America to help catch her rapist also meant her child would be born a US citizen. God always has a plan, she'd tell Cassie when Cassie took her to her OB appointments. He knows something bad can be turned into something good if you have faith in Him.

Cassie had always suffered from a lack of faith—until she met Alina, witnessed firsthand her faith in action. She hadn't told anyone, not even Drake, but Alina's faith was what had sustained her these past few months, helped Cassie get past her own rage at a faceless God who gave life, but then took it away without warning.

"No one at ICE would say where she was," Drake told them. "They wouldn't even admit to detaining her. They had no record of her anywhere. Believe me, I pulled in every favor I could, trying to find her."

"She just...vanished," Cassie finished for him. "Three months, no sign of her. Until four days ago. When they found her body."

"You think they weren't ICE?" TK asked. "That it was the rapist."

"Then he has a partner," Wash put in. "There were two men who took her."

"That's assuming the two attacks were related, and it wasn't just some random stalk-pregnant-women-to-steal-their-baby nutjob," TK said. "Like that lady in Texas whose best friend threw her a baby shower, only it wasn't, and she kidnapped her, planning to kill the mom after the baby was born."

"Those cases are almost always women suffering severe psychiatric illness," Wash argued. "Our best bet is the men who took Alina are associated with the rapist."

Lucy folded both hands around the stack of photos in front of her. She was frowning, but also nodding. Cassie knew she'd made up her mind.

"Whoever took Alina held her for three months," Lucy said. "Which means we finally have an active crime scene if we can locate it. We need to know where she was held, how she got away, why she was naked on that bridge, and where her baby is now."

Cassie's breath escaped her—she hadn't even realized she'd been holding it. She squeezed Drake's hand. She'd promised Alina she'd look after her baby if anything happened. Now, maybe, she had the chance to keep that promise. For a brief moment, she imagined the weight of a sleeping child in her arms, the warmth of his breath against her cheek.

Alina's baby was still alive. He had to be.

Chapter 5

Less than twenty minutes in and Lucy already despised this case. A predator torturing, then drugging his victim, stealing her memories? Taking a pregnant woman and holding her until her baby was born? That last hit especially close to home. Her final case with the FBI had involved a serial pedophile, known as Daddy, who'd kidnapped pregnant women in order to keep and raise their baby girls, groom them to fulfill his every twisted need. Once he was done with the mothers, he'd killed them. Once the babies had grown too old for him, he'd sold them to other men with similar depraved tastes.

Daddy was dead, she reminded herself. This couldn't be him.

Which somehow made it worse. How many sick psychopaths were out there, preying on women and children? It was the one thing she'd hated about her job with the FBI, the endless game of whack-a-mole that the good guys were destined to forever lose.

"I still don't see how you all can be so sure the

baby is still alive," TK argued.

"If he wanted to destroy the evidence, he could have killed Alina and the baby at any time," Lucy said. "But he kept her alive long enough to give birth. No, he wants or needs the baby." She paused, her voice tightening. "A rapist who wants a child."

"Why?" Wash asked. "To sell, like, to a black-market adoption ring?"

"Or to raise," Lucy answered, her words coming slowly. "Keep for himself."

Hart made a small noise at that, and Drake grew rigid, his gaze circling the room as if searching for a threat he could physically fight.

"How old was Alina?" Lucy asked. The answer was in the file before her, but she couldn't look at those photos again. Not the images of the abuse Alina had suffered. Lucy could compartmentalize that, shut it away with the other horrors she'd seen and experienced over the years. No, it was the headshot from the modeling agency she dreaded. A young girl, her gaze filled with hope, eager to embrace her future.

That photo was the one that broke Lucy's heart. How many times had she seen that same expression on Megan, her teenage daughter?

It was why Hart had brought paper documents, Lucy knew. It wasn't a lack of technology; it was because Hart knew this might be a hard case to sell to her audience. Smart woman.

"She only turned nineteen last month," Hart answered.

A heavy silence fell over the room.

Lucy glanced at Wash, who nodded back, his fingers stretched wide, ready to unleash them on his keyboard. But TK avoided Lucy's gaze. Although Lucy had the ultimate decision on whether they took a case, she needed her team on board to get the job done, so she sat back and let TK ask her questions.

"Where do we even start?" TK's tone was grudging. "If we're saying the baby was alive—is alive—he could be anywhere by now. Whoever took him might not live here in Pittsburgh or Allegheny County," she argued. "Or even the state—it's a short drive to Ohio, West Virginia, Maryland, New York." She slumped back, rocking her chair hard, turning her glare on Lucy. "Why don't you tell them what we're really up against here?"

"She's right. Looking for the baby isn't the answer." Lucy didn't mind TK—it was Wash's look of disappointment that was difficult to take. Somedays she forgot just how young he was. He met her gaze for a brief moment, then lowered his face, his fingers toying with one of the many rubber finger-sized monsters suctioned around the frame of his monitor. This one was a blue Dalek—the epitome of fascism, defeated only by self-sacrifice and the nobility of the human heart. Nick had tried to explain that to her during one of his many attempts to get her excited about Doctor Who.

"Then what is?" Wash challenged her, aiming the Dalek's eyestalk at her.

"We need to find the rapist." Lucy paused, glancing at each of them, especially Drake, who must have come to the same conclusion—probably even before he came here, seeking their help. "Because he's done this before. He won't risk leaving evidence behind again. He'll kill his next victim."

TK finally opened the folder in front of her. "He won't stop. He enjoys it too much." Her voice was a low murmur, her gaze fixed on the photos. "Playing God, destroying lives."

"Does that make him unstoppable?" Hart asked, her tone resigned.

"No. It means he'll slip up." Lucy hated glamorizing serials. It gave them too much power and allure, when in reality they were most often ordinary men living ordinary lives—men able to be hunted themselves, not the larger-than-life Hannibal Lecters Hollywood made them out to be. "The more his fantasy life intrudes on reality, he'll get angry, or overexcited, move too fast, or choose the wrong victim. Because, as much as he enjoys playing God, he's still just a man."

To her surprise, TK was the first to voice her agreement. "Just a man," she echoed. "Human and vulnerable like his victims." She finally met Lucy's gaze, although her expression was more haunted than determined. She jerked her chin in a quick nod.

Lucy stood. "Dr. Hart, if you and TK could go over Alina's interviews, look for any clues. Build us a profile of this guy. Wash, search the area around the courthouse for any videos taken near the time Alina was abducted. Maybe we'll get lucky."

"So, you'll take the case?" Hart asked eagerly.

"We'll take the case." She gestured to Drake. "You're with me. Anyone in the DEA owe you a favor?"

He scraped his chair back and stood, obviously reluctant to leave his wife. "No. Why?"

"Don't worry, I have an in."

"To what?"

"Tracking our designer date-rape drug. And with it, maybe finding more victims."

That caught his attention. She strode through the door, Drake rushing to catch up. "You know we looked, so did the Staties. We didn't find anyone," he said in a low tone, glancing back at the room where his wife was. Not wanting to disappoint her. Lucy liked that about him.

"Doesn't mean they aren't out there," Lucy said. "Or that he didn't make any mistakes. We just need to cast a wider net." She slid her phone from her pocket. "And I know the perfect fisherman. C'mon."

Chapter 6

THERE WAS A GOOD CHANCE Oshiro was stalking his next target, so Lucy began with a text. To her surprise, he responded by calling back just as she and Drake reached the parking lot. "Lucy in the stars with diamonds. How are you, girl?"

"Little Timmy Oshiro, I need a favor."

"Shoot. Not like I don't owe you about forty-seven. Thousand."

"Got anyone at the DEA whose arm you could twist? I need a database lookup."

His low rumble of a chuckle echoed through the phone loud enough that Drake looked over. "Oh yeah, I do. I'll text you where to park. Whatcha driving?"

She glanced at Drake, who had his car keys out and was getting ready to open the driver's door on a classic Mustang. Not exactly inconspicuous. Given that Oshiro and his team's lives depended on keeping a low profile, she shook her head at Drake and nodded to her Subaru. "The Forester."

"Perfect." Here in Pittsburgh, Subarus were

second only to gray Hondas as the perfect blend-into-the-scenery undercover vehicles. "I'll meet you there." Oshiro hung up.

Lucy got into the Subaru, and Drake joined her. "Where we headed?"

She handed him her phone as Oshiro's text chimed. "Looks like a back alley, Hill District."

He squinted at the phone as she drove. "Sat view shows a mix of commercial and residential. One of those older neighborhoods where you used to be able to walk to shops, a church on every block." He took out his own phone, no doubt accessing the police database. Then he gave a low whistle. "Can't remember the last time I saw this many warrants tied to a single city block."

Lucy wasn't surprised. "Deputy US Marshal Timothy Oshiro runs the Western PA Fugitive Apprehension Strike Team. He likes settling into a neighborhood, then rounding up a bunch of targets at once."

"Your fisherman. Casting an especially large net."

"That's Timmy. Nothing small about the man."

They crossed the river and headed over to Bryn Mawr Road, which, despite its name, had nothing about it reminiscent of the upscale Philly suburb. The once-stately prewar homes were surrounded by weeds and empty lots, many of them suffering from the ravages of time. The few commercial buildings were shuttered and covered in graffiti, and the only viable enterprises Lucy noted were the churches that sat on almost every block—although even those were sheltered behind wrought-iron fences with sturdy gates.

X marked the coordinates Oshiro had sent them, but it was no treasure trove. Rather, a small loading zone semi-concealed between two industrial-sized dumpsters down an alley behind an abandoned furniture store. Lucy backed the Subaru in; from the street, it would be difficult to see unless you walked right up to it. Which told her a lot about what Oshiro and his team were up to.

A sharp rap on the passenger side window had Drake reaching for his weapon. He was a southpaw like Lucy, she noticed, even as she smothered her laughter. A large bald man had pressed his face against Drake's window; his not very well-groomed face, dark beard bristling, eyebrows tousled. "Wash your window? One dolla, one dolla."

"No, thanks," Drake snapped.

Lucy stepped out of the car and circled around to the disheveled man, embracing him in a bear hug. Thankfully, his raggedy clothing was cleaner than its appearance suggested. He responded by lifting her off the ground and swinging her around before setting her down in the shadows of the loading area they'd appropriated. "Good to see you, Lucy-Mae. Let's boogie."

Drake opened his door and joined them, his hand still under his coat, resting casually near his weapon.

"Who's the nervous Nellie?" Oshiro asked.

Drake answered for himself. "Drake, Major Crimes."

Lucy didn't bother watching the two men do their sizing up. She'd seen it too many times before. At least when women did their similar judgy-judgy hierarchal assessment, they didn't stop everything, assuming the world would simply pause and wait until they decided who was alpha. She glanced around the dimly lit alcove. Given the decaying trash, the peeling paint beneath layers of graffiti, and the bent, rusted aluminum signs, the furniture store had been a long time abandoned.

Oshiro led the way through the scattered debris—a burnt mattress, several broken chairs, a tower of wood pallets—and approached a metal door nestled into the far side of the area. The faint outline of the words staff only could still be deciphered if Lucy squinted. He rapped, and the door opened, revealing an equally disheveled Hispanic man holding a Glock at the ready. With a nod from Oshiro, he holstered his weapon and held the door open as Lucy and Drake sidled through it.

"Don't forget to save me some bacon," the man said as he locked the door behind them. They were in a small hallway with a staircase to their left and an office, its door open, in front of them. Inside the office was an array of monitoring equipment. From the number of images, Oshiro must have ringed most of the block with cameras.

"The bacon," Oshiro exclaimed, sprinting up the stairs with more grace than a man his size should possess. That was Oshiro, a wealth of contradictions.

"Seriously," the man said to Lucy. "Man makes a killer BLT."

"I'll make sure he doesn't forget you," Lucy assured him as he returned to his observation post. She began up the steps, Drake following. Sure enough, once they passed the first landing, the smell of bacon guided them the rest of the way. The three-story building had apartments on the second and third floors, although there was no sign of any current occupants, not until they reached the top floor, the scent of bacon enticing them past vacant apartments to the front of the building, where a door stood open in invitation.

Lucy crossed the threshold, stepping into what would have been the living room. The space itself was as decrepit as the rest of the building—plaster walls peeling from rot and mildew, ceiling splotched with water stains, the smell of decay competing with the aroma of bacon. Two air mattresses were shoved against the far wall. A cluster of stadium chairs faced the large windows surrounded by an array of surveillance equipment. One of the chairs was occupied by a man dressed in a baggy Steelers sweatshirt, holding binoculars with one hand and a radio with the other.

"In here," Oshiro called. Lucy and Drake drifted from the living area into the dining room, where a folding table was covered with laptops and paperwork. More chairs sat near the windows. Another man, this one wearing a black hoodie, sat at the table hunched over a monitor, a joystick in his hand.

Lucy turned into the kitchen that opened onto the dining area. Oshiro had donned a pair of pink flamingo oven mitts and was removing a pan from the oven. Beside him stood a tall, thin black man wearing a UNC basketball jersey, watching his every move.

"So once you add the shredded red cabbage to the bacon, you let it kinda crisp and caramelize in the bacon fat, then you take them both out and put the bread in." Oshiro matched words with deeds, scooping what had to be two pounds of crisp, juicy bacon and equally crisp cabbage off the pan and onto a platter lined with paper towels, while his cooking partner took slices of thick, dark bread and carefully arranged them on the greasy pan. Oshiro nodded his approval, slid the pan into the oven, fussed with the settings, then handed off his oven mitts to the other man. "Watch it doesn't burn. The bread and tomatoes should be done about the same time."

The man nodded as if accepting a sacred duty. "Got it."

"Pretty luxe stakeout," Lucy said. "In my day, we lived in our cars and ate cold fast food."

Drake was more interested in the man at the table beside them. "Is that a drone?"

Oshiro chuckled. "Amazing what kind of toys you can get when you drop the words 'national security' into a target package."

"Nice." Drake nodded as he watched over the drone operator's shoulder.

"Enough about work," Lucy said. "How are June

and the baby?"

Oshiro's smile widened, revealing all his teeth. That smile was known to break hardened criminals, but that was only because they didn't know what a soft heart lay behind the bulk. "Got new pictures." He pulled out his cell phone. As Lucy scrolled along the photo stream of June and her baby girl, she couldn't help but think of Alina. Her hopeful smile. Her baby. All gone now.

Oshiro sensed her shift in emotions. "Tig here is your DEA guy." He nodded to the man juggling a pan of roasted grape tomatoes, their skins bursting with sweet juices, and the pan of now-toasted bread, as he assembled the sandwiches. "Tig, this is Lucy Guardino, former FBI. She needs your help, so you give her anything she wants, got it?"

Tig, who on closer inspection, maybe actually was old enough to shave, smiled and nodded, handing Oshiro the tongs and trading positions with him in the narrow kitchen. He joined Lucy at the table. "Whatcha need?"

No questions, no arguments, no debates about agency jurisdiction or her lack of authority—that was the kind of loyalty Oshiro commanded. Lucy felt a pang of regret, thinking of her team at the FBI. Once upon a time, they'd looked at her just like Tig looked at Oshiro.

"Drake's a PPB detective," she told Tig, giving him some administrative cover. "And I'm now a licensed PI working for the Beacon Group."

"Yeah, I've heard of you guys. Just like I've

heard of you, Ms. Guardino. They still teach your geographic profiling unit at Quantico. And how you used it to catch Clinton Caine." His expression of awe made Lucy feel old and drew a guffaw of smothered laughter from Oshiro behind her.

Oshiro brought paper plates with still-steaming sandwiches to her and Drake. "Guests first," he said when the drone operator glanced up and started to say something. "Help yourself to drinks from the fridge. Or the coffee if you're feeling particularly brave."

Drake stood to grab drinks as Oshiro delivered plates to everyone else and sent the man from the front room downstairs with another plate for their teammate, leaving Tig, Lucy, and Drake at the table with the silent drone operator.

"We have a rape case," Drake started, ignoring his sandwich. Lucy didn't have his willpower. She crunched down on the aromatic construction, while he explained about Alina. "The crime lab ID'd the drugs used on her, said they'd never seen them before."

Lucy swallowed and wiped her hands on a paper towel. Despite the bacon, the bacon-crisped cabbage, and the bread fried on one side, Oshiro's take on the BLT wasn't greasy at all. No wonder his team was so loyal, if he fed them like this. "I thought you could run it through the DEA lab's database of illicit drugs. Maybe we could get a handle on where it came from. Or find more victims outside Allegheny County."

"No problem. Let me just set up the search." Tig clicked on a laptop, screens flashing past. Then he sat back. His sandwich had long since vanished. He looked longingly past her to the kitchen. Drake took the hint and slid his own plate in front of Tig. "Sure?" he asked Drake, who nodded. Tig squashed the sandwich between both hands and practically inhaled it. "Next time I see my momma, I'm gonna teach her how to make this for sure."

"Where're you from?" Lucy asked. Because of their undercover work, DEA agents often rotated far away from their homes.

"Charlotte, North Carolina. But I busted some Bloods and got a green light." A no-holds-barred hit put out by gangs. "So now I get to freeze my butt up here for the time being." His computer chirped. "No hits on manufacturers or anyone busted for possession of your mystery drug, but I think you have a problem."

"What's that?" Drake asked, leaning forward to see the screen.

"You don't have one victim. You've got seven."

Chapter 7

Cassie glanced across the table, toward the open doorway of Lucy's team's office. She wished she could have gone with Drake and Lucy. At least they got to do something. Instead, she got stuck sitting here being grilled by a former Marine who must have been a drill sergeant—as if Cassie were the one who'd kidnapped Alina.

"Look again," TK instructed. "What was this guy doing?" She aimed a laser pointer at a frozen film frame of a man starting up the courthouse steps. "Did you see where he came from?"

Wash had been able to find only a handful of video clips from the area around the courthouse that morning, mostly from tourists or people at the courthouse getting married, since actual security video had long ago been overwritten. Now they were going over each clip frame by frame, trying to look for clues about Alina's captors.

"C'mon, Cassie," TK urged, shifting gears from drill instructor to cheerleader. Cassie wondered if TK also played both roles of good cop and bad cop when she'd been interrogating suspects for the Marines. "You must have seen something. Try again." She motioned to Wash to re-run the clip. "This guy, focus on him. Where did he come from?"

"I told you," Cassie snapped. "I don't know." Her glare had no effect on the former Marine. "Why does it matter? He was nowhere near the street when Alina was taken." She slumped back in her chair, pressing both palms against her eyes. "None of it matters. She's gone."

Despite her closed eyes, she could practically see the silent conversation that TK and Wash were having. TK was moving her hands—Cassie felt the rush of air—and Wash thumped his wheelchair, refusing whatever she wanted. Another tense interval of motionless silence—TK trying to stare Wash into submission no doubt—and then the sound of Wash rolling his chair across the wood floor.

Cassie opened her eyes. TK was across the room, chomping on a slice of the pizza they'd gotten for lunch, chewing fast, as if it were a tasteless MRE, and Wash had sidled up beside Cassie. He was even younger than she'd first thought, she realized.

"It all matters," he told her in a soft voice. The voice of someone who'd been in the same position she was. "I remember how you feel. When I got shot—I was twelve, it was a gang drive-by—the cops kept asking me over and over about the car, about the driver, about the shooter. I couldn't tell them anything. Not because I didn't want to. Because all I could see when I tried to remember anything wasn't the car or the gun or the guy pulling the trigger." He held her gaze, but his expression turned sorrowful. "It wasn't even me getting shot, the noise, the pain, the fear. No, all I could see was my baby sister going down, the blood where her face once was. All I could remember was how shocked and angry and sad and..."

He glanced away, not at TK but out the open door as if he wished he were anywhere but here, as if he wished he was back in time, in that moment—or better yet, the moment before. "And all I could think, hammering in my brain over and over, was that it was all my fault. She was dead because I wanted to get a stupid comic book. I just had to get it that day, knew they'd be arriving at the store, and I couldn't wait for my mom to get off work, so I took her with me. One minute, I was laughing at one of her stupid knock-knock jokes, and the next..."

He swallowed hard. "The next, we were both on the ground, lying in our own blood, and I couldn't move, I couldn't even try to help her. She was just out of reach. The only thing I could reach, as hard as I tried, was her blood. There was so much blood."

Silence filled the room. Even TK had stopped chewing, staring at Wash. Cassie realized this must be the first time TK had heard Wash's story.

Cassie blinked hard, choking back tears. "Thank you." She skipped past pointless platitudes that would mean nothing coming from a stranger. "You're right. Every time I look at these videos and see Alina being taken, I can't think. I just feel guilty. I'm the one who convinced her to let her rape kit be submitted, to go to the police in the first place. Over eighty percent of victims never even report a sexual assault, but I talked Alina into it. And I'm the one who came up with the idea of using the baby's DNA when the rape kit came back negative for any other evidence."

She blew her breath out, forced her clenched fists to open. "I'm the one who thought if the DA met her, saw her, then he'd go the extra mile. I told Alina to meet me there that morning. And then, when she was taken—" She shook her head, anger flooding her. "I was so stupid. How the hell could I have not seen that they weren't real ICE agents? It's my fault she's dead." She glanced at the doorway again, ready to bolt if Wash's chair hadn't been blocking her path. The urge to run was overwhelming. But not as strong as her need to make things right again. For Alina. For Alina's son.

"It's all my fault." She straightened in her seat. "Run it again, back before that man shows up." Then she turned to TK. "Why are you so interested in that man, anyway?"

TK abandoned what remained of her pizza and walked to the whiteboard on the far wall, where the image was still frozen. "Because he's the only one we've seen who pulls out his cell phone and uses it right after Alina shows up." She tapped her finger to the far edge of the frame where a woman's shadow— Alina—had just appeared.

Cassie stood up, leaning across the table to see better. Wash returned to his computer, rewinding the video and running it again in slow motion. "I didn't even see her there. I never even noticed her, not until she was farther down the block, ready to cross the street."

"But he did. See where he's looking? The couple throwing the wedding bouquet is distracting you, distracting everyone, but not this guy. This guy has eyes only for Alina. And he's texting someone something at the same time. See him typing on his phone?"

"He's the lookout," Cassie said. "If we can find him—"

"We'll be one step closer to finding Alina's killer. And her baby."

"AT LEAST YOUR ACTOR isn't flooding the streets with this shit," Oshiro said as he walked them back to Lucy's car.

"If he was, the DEA might have noticed sooner," Lucy said, not bothering to hide the resentment in her voice. Not that it was the DEA's fault. They were targeting major criminal enterprises and drug cartels, not some homegrown chemist mixing up batches in his basement. Still... "I guess seven women with their lives ruined is just a statistical error in the war on drugs."

"It's crossed jurisdictions. Maybe a task force? Could go federal if you got the right people interested." Except the right people were Lucy and her old task force—the one the FBI had deemed redundant and unnecessary.

Drake was behind them, talking on his phone to the Pittsburgh sex crimes detective working Alina's case. He hung up just as they reached the Subaru. "Carter's reaching out to the departments that submitted the other drug samples."

The DEA had logged only the samples and the jurisdictions they came from, so there was no information about individual cases.

"If there's a pattern of open cases similar to Alina's, then she'll start a VICAP profile. Not sure what more we can do now. It all depends on what the other cases show."

"You saw the list." Lucy clicked the remote to unlock the car. "Pittsburgh is the only major city. The rest are all small towns scattered between West Virginia, Maryland, Ohio." A thought struck her, something Tig had said about her research in geographic profiling. "But I'll bet if we map them out, none of them occurred in unincorporated areas."

"What's that got to do with anything?" Drake asked.

Oshiro waved a hand at him. "Shut up and let her work her magic."

"I'll know more once I get a map and more info about the other jurisdictions," Lucy said. Drake didn't seem satisfied with her answer, but she needed more facts before she could be certain of anything.

Oshiro bundled Lucy into his arms, kissing her on the top of her head. "That's from June and the baby." Then he held her at arm's length, staring at her with an earnest expression. "You need anything, you call."

She frowned. "Technically, we can't get involved unless the other jurisdictions invite us."

He shook his head, tossing her doubts aside.

"You'll find a way. You always do. You're gonna nail this bastard, Lucy. I feel it in my bones." He started to walk away but turned back, squaring his shoulders as he assumed a patrol sergeant's persona. "Let's be careful out there."

"You need to stop spending your stakeouts watching old cop shows." But his perfect Hill Street Blues impression had lightened her mood. She and Drake climbed into the car and began driving back to Beacon Falls.

"Tig said you taught at Quantico?" Drake asked.

"When I was part of the Critical Incident Response Group. Taught FBI, DEA, National Academy. Mainly geographic profiling, because that's what I did my research in, but also forensic interviewing and hostage negotiation tactics."

"So did you ever work as a profiler with the BAU?" The Behavioral Analysis Unit, the FBI's prestigious profiling unit.

"No. I took their courses, but I mainly hung out with the HRT guys." She smiled at the memory. The FBI's elite Hostage Rescue Team was the equivalent of a police department's SWAT team, only they responded to critical incidents all over the country. "Roping out of helicopters was tons more fun than being stuck in a windowless room crunching data."

"But those serial killers you've caught, that was through your geoprofiling? That's why you think where the drugs were reported is important."

"It's a tool. But think about it. In small towns without their own police departments and in unincorporated rural areas, who'd handle a case like Alina's?"

"Here, it'd be the Pennsylvania State Police. Other states, probably county sheriffs. They'd have the resources to do a proper investigation."

"Exactly. But a town with a population just large enough to have a police department—even if it's just a few officers—they're always going to be short on manpower and budget. A lot of them won't even have a detective, but it doesn't look good if they're constantly calling in the State Police or whoever, so unless it's a big, splashy homicide—"

"Odds are they'll work it themselves." He straightened in his seat. "Which means sending tox screens and, maybe, if they have the budget, running a rape kit—although testing it might wait until they have a suspect."

"Plus, asking a few questions—mostly about the victim, because what else would they have to go on?"

"Honestly, even with our Sex Crimes Unit specializing in cases like Alina's, they couldn't do a whole lot more, given the lack of evidence."

"Still. I think he made a mistake coming here." She made a left turn onto Centre Avenue, taking a slight detour, but he didn't object. After all, until the other jurisdictions got back to them, there really wasn't much for Lucy and Drake to do. "Or, maybe after six successful attacks—"

"That we know of."

"That we know of. Maybe he's gotten so comfortable that he didn't see it as a risk, finding a victim here in a city with a well-staffed police department. Or maybe convenience outweighed the risk." She turned down Baum, then slowed to a crawl until she saw the alley she was looking for. The one where Alina had been found nine months ago. Lucy drove down it slowly, observing the vantage points—or lack thereof—and any security. Or lack thereof.

On the corner was an auto shop, providing overhangs and covered drive-throughs to the various repair areas. Backing onto the alley on the other side were fenced-in yards and parking areas for a variety of multifamily housing units. Behind the auto shop was the dumpster, tucked into a concrete alcove, where Alina had been found. If the mechanics had arrived for work an hour later, she probably would have died, but they started early in the morning, responding to commuter breakdowns.

Lucy parked the car in front of the dumpster and got out. The alcove kept the dumpster hidden from the view of the apartment residents. A narrow drive led from the alley out to St. Clair Street, totally covered by the larger building on the other side of the auto shop. She walked down the alley, shivering as wind trapped by the narrow walls of the urban canyon whistled past. The building had been constructed to provide its occupants with covered parking along with easy access from the streets on both sides. But there were no lights on, leaving the area in almost complete darkness even now in the early afternoon. And no security cameras. He could have pulled in off the street, kept his vehicle hidden inside the covered parking area, dumped Alina beside the garbage, and been gone within seconds without anyone ever seeing or hearing him.

Their actor knew the area. Intimately. No way in hell would a guy this sophisticated depend on luck to find such a perfect dump site.

She reached the front door of the building. It was currently vacant and, from the dust covering the floor inside the lobby, had been for some time. She peered through the grime-covered glass at the faded sign over the reception desk. Vigilant Security Consultants.

Lucy rattled the locked door in frustration. "Son of a bitch has a sense of humor."

Drake's gaze swiveled back and forth, and she knew he was seeing the same details she was. He glanced at the sign, grimacing. "He lives here."

"Or works here, was raised here. But yeah. He knows Pittsburgh. It's his home territory."

"Territory," he echoed. "As in hunting grounds."

"As in, he's getting cocky. He's going to strike again."

CHAPTER 9

BY THE TIME LUCY and Drake arrived back at Beacon Falls, they still hadn't heard anything from Carter, the detective handling Alina's case. Lucy parked the car, and they trudged up the path and into the house in silence. If her theory was correct, then the other cases were all being investigated by overworked, understaffed, small-town agencies, where sharing info with a big-city cop might not be a priority. Especially as, to those small departments, these crimes were not only cold cases, but they also represented failures. Even if they wanted outside help, they'd also need to get the permission of their victims—who might balk at the idea of strangers intruding into their private hell.

Once inside the foyer, Drake passed her, practically sprinting up the steps as if he owned the place. Eager to see his wife, Lucy thought. Or eager to retrieve Hart and leave Alina's case far behind—along with the ugly truth that a serial predator was on the loose.

She reached her team's office two steps behind him. To her surprise, he'd already reclaimed his seat beside Hart. So they were staying, at least for the time being. Maybe the reluctance she sensed from Drake was more about protecting his wife than avoiding this case. She could understand that. How many times had she unwittingly placed her own family in the crosshairs because she'd been too focused on a case instead of the possible consequences to them?

"We got something," TK said as soon as Lucy crossed the threshold. "There weren't two men who took Alina. There were three." She rushed behind Lucy to close the door and, before Lucy even reached her seat, clicked the lights off. "Watch."

A couple ran out the courthouse doors, surrounded by friends and family, obviously just married. The bride wore a pale gold dress that shimmered in the sunlight and carried a bouquet that she tossed into the laughing crowd.

Then the video froze. "See this guy?" TK pointed to a man with his back to the camera as he climbed the sun-drenched granite steps toward the courthouse entrance. He wore a conservative suit but didn't carry a briefcase or any files like a lawyer would. TK nodded to Wash, and the video resumed. The man stopped and turned away from the courthouse doors until he faced the street. He glanced up, then glanced down and used his phone.

"He's just spotted Alina." TK pointed to the silhouette of a pregnant woman moving into the frame. "And he's texting his partners to come grab her."

Since the video was focused on the wedding party, the man's face was caught in only a few frames as the bouquet flew into the air. But he looked vaguely familiar.

"Slow it down, zoom in on him," Lucy told Wash, excited by the prospect of a lead.

The video replayed, frame by frame, until the man's face came into focus for one brief moment. Lucy almost laughed when she saw who it was. "That's not a lookout," she told them. "That's the Homeland Security investigator working with the US attorney. Name's Jared Estanza. He's probably in and out of the courthouse a few times a week."

"Are you sure?" TK asked, appearing crestfallen. "I mean, look at him, the timing." Wash ran the sequence again. "He turns deliberately toward the street, looks right at Alina, then texts someone, and the SUV appears." She slumped into her chair. "It doesn't make sense."

"Maybe they really are ICE?" Hart asked. "Maybe Jared Estanza was calling them—" She cut off, her logic unspooling. "No, that makes no sense. Why would the US attorney get involved in an expired-visa case? It's not like Alina was a terrorist."

"Play it again," Drake said, standing to peer at the whiteboard as the video played out. Then he chuckled. "Lucy's right. Estanza has nothing to do with Alina. Rewind it." Wash did as ordered. "Stop there." The image froze just as Estanza pivoted away from the courthouse and back toward the street. "See his phone in his hand? Look at how the shadows are falling. Estanza turned around so the sun would be behind him and he could read his phone's screen without any glare. That's all. And see?" He motioned to Wash to resume. "He sends his text, then turns back and continues up the steps."

"And that guy he joins up with..." Lucy pointed to a man's profile, barely visible in a single frame. "I think that's Graham Hunt, the US attorney."

"So he's not our guy." Wash rocked his chair in frustration. "Dammit, that was the best lead we had."

"The guys dressed as ICE agents, did they show up in any of the videos?" Lucy asked.

"Nope. This one caught the van arriving. It's as close as we got."

The room filled with the gloom of disappointment. That's how cases like this were—one step forward, two back. "Drake and I found something." She told them about the other victims. "Detective Carter from the Sex Crimes Unit is waiting to hear back from the other jurisdictions."

"So are we even still on the case?" TK asked.

Drake answered. "The Beacon Group and PPB already have a working relationship, and Carter says she doesn't mind the help. They just cut her team by half, so she's drowning in open cases. She also did one of your sexual assault felony trainings." He nodded to Lucy. "Guess you made an impression."

"What about Alina's statement?" Lucy stood and flicked the lights back on. Then she grabbed a dry erase marker and approached the whiteboard. "We can start building a profile, flesh it out once we hear about the other victims."

"We know he doesn't work alone," TK said. "Two men grabbed Alina."

Hart straightened at that. "That kinda echoes something Alina said in her first interview. That she thought there were two attackers." She turned to Wash. "It's the interview from the ICU, so audio only. I think around the ten-minute mark."

He nodded, and a few minutes later Hart's disembodied voice sounded from the computer's speakers, accompanied by the background noise of a busy ICU. "We don't have to talk about what he did to you. Not yet, not until you're ready. Let's focus on where you were, Alina. I know you were blindfolded, but was there anything you heard, anything you smelled? Just the first thing that comes to mind."

"The man, he crazy man," came a young woman's halting voice. She sounded raspy, hoarse. Lucy remembered how sore her own throat had been when they'd removed the breathing tube after she'd woken up in the ICU. "He talked to himself. All the time. Never to me—"

"Was someone else there?" A second woman's voice. Rushed, eager. "Alina, was there more than one man who attacked you?"

"That's Carter," Drake told them.

Hart shook her head, almost rolling her eyes as there was a pause in the taped conversation. "And that's me telling her not to push the witness."

Then Alina's voice returned with her accented

English. "I can't remember another man talking. All the time just him. But maybe two men, yes. One, he touch my hair, so soft. The other—" A muffled sob. "He angry, so angry. Hit me. Hurt me. Then first one, he sad, crying, said he had no choice. I think maybe angry man boss of him?"

Lucy felt her face go cold. "Stop there."

"What is it, boss?" Wash asked.

It couldn't be... Could it?

"What she described..." Lucy faltered. "Three years ago, we busted a sex trafficking ring," she told them. "They held women captive, livestreamed everything, took bids from customers who scripted what happened to them or paid to do whatever they wanted." Her grand jury case from this morning—ICE had deported their witnesses before they could testify. Two men dressed as ICE agents had grabbed Alina. "Maybe the first man was Alina's captor, but the violent one was a paying client?"

"It's not an uncommon business practice," Wash said. "Even street gangs are turning to trafficking instead of drugs. Safer, cheaper, and the men almost never do jail time. It's always the women who are arrested."

"You think it's the same actors?" Drake asked, cutting to the heart of the matter. "Or a new crew borrowing the same business model?"

They all turned to Lucy, but she didn't answer, not right away. To buy time, she paced past the whiteboard, ending up staring out the window but ignoring the vista made brilliant by the bright fall colors. It couldn't be the same ring. They'd have to be fools to start up again, taking women from the street, operating right here in Pittsburgh, where their case was going before a grand jury.

Fools...or men so powerful they knew they could get away with anything. Men without remorse. Men without fear.

Men who would stop at nothing. Men above the law. Or a man above the law—rich, powerful, more popular than Santa Claus. Hunt's target.

She turned back to her team. "I need to reach out to a few people, go over Alina's interviews myself. And any info we get on the other victims. Let's stop here for the day, regroup in the morning."

Wash and TK nodded, trusting her judgment. Drake was already halfway to the door, guiding Hart away from what Lucy knew he sensed was a viper's pit of a case. She didn't blame him. Hart's lone victim had grown to seven victims, an orchestrated kidnapping right in front of the courthouse in broad daylight, actors who knew how to use law enforcement jurisdictions against them...and a missing baby.

One day in and this case was already spiraling out of control. The last time that had happened, it hadn't been only Lucy who had paid the price—her team and her family had also been caught in the deadly crossfire.

But then Hart turned back, looking past Drake to meet Lucy's gaze. "But you're not giving up, right? We're still going to find Alina's baby. We need you. You all have done more in a day than we've been able to do in months. You can't quit, not now."

Despite his wife's pleading, the expression Drake aimed at Lucy was one of fierce protectiveness. He didn't need words to echo Lucy's feelings—he didn't want anyone he cared for anywhere near this case. Because, like Lucy, he knew just how bad it could get.

"I won't give up," Lucy promised Hart. "See you tomorrow."

Drake's frown deepened. "Carter will take it from here. Hart won't be coming back."

Hart bristled at that, ready to argue. She ignored her husband to focus on Lucy. "I will see you tomorrow." Then she stalked away, leaving Drake behind.

Chapter 10

DESPITE DRAKE'S BEST ATTEMPTS, Hart's frosty silence lasted the entire drive to their building in East Liberty. He'd barely parked the car when she bounded out, bypassing the entrance to the community clinic she'd built and oversaw—which told him exactly how upset she was—and jogged up the stairs leading to their apartment on the top floor. He ran after her but hung back when she paused at the door to the third floor, bowing her head and listening for a long moment.

Behind the door lay the center's day care and preschool. Where the laughter of children filled the air, their joyful noise singing through the door. He reached the landing, took a tentative step toward her, the ancient oak floorboards creaking beneath his weight. Her back still to him, she shook her head and turned to climb the remaining steps to their home.

He followed, her silence a heavy weight that slowed his pace. She'd left the door open, and he closed it, set the alarm. The spacious living area of the renovated loft was empty, as was his studio and their bedroom.

He found her waiting in the former guest room, now painted a vivid dandelion yellow with bright jungle murals covering the walls. He'd moved the crib and the changing table and the animal mobile into storage months ago, but she'd insisted that he leave the matching rocking chairs. It'd been over five months, but still she'd sit in here—usually with the lights off—almost every night before coming to bed.

Drake stifled his sigh, took the seat beside her, and reached out his hand. She didn't take it, not right away, but finally, she intertwined her fingers in his as they rocked side by side. As much as he wanted to explain, to comfort, yes, even to argue, he'd learned the hard way that Hart did things in her own time. Pressing her to face a problem before she was ready resulted only in a frustrating shouting match—and him sleeping on the couch.

When they'd first met, their confrontations—he didn't think of them as fights since usually they were on the same side, and always they ended up closer afterward—sparked some of the best sex he'd ever had. After studying Hart, learning what drove her, he realized that although sometimes she needed to explode, let all her combustible emotions burn off, usually she only wanted time and patience. Two qualities he'd been in short supply of when they first met, but being with her...it made it worth learning how to wait.

After a few minutes, she squeezed his hand,

stood, and led him from the room. She closed the door behind them, pulling it shut with a gentle click of the latch, her hand resting on the doorknob for a moment as if she was reluctant to leave. They stepped back into the living area, the large Amish-crafted dining table before them, the twin leather sofas beyond it, the well-appointed kitchen beside them.

Drake waited to see which direction she'd choose. Turning right into the kitchen would mean a companionable discussion over dinner. Walking past the dining table to the more open area of the living room, where she'd have space to pace as she made her arguments, would mean he'd pissed her off pretty damn thoroughly.

Or, his favorite option—if anyone asked him: keep going through the living room into their bedroom, where they could turn anger and frustration into passion.

"Cassie," he said, using her first name—their special code for intimacy—hoping to tempt her into the third choice, bypass the argument altogether. "I'm—"

She whirled on him as if his words had triggered an IED. "Don't. Don't even."

He stepped closer, holding her gaze, trying to breach her emotions. But she knew exactly what he was doing. She turned her back and stalked around the dining table, placing it between them as she paced the area between the table and the couch, inching ever closer to the front door and escape. For Hart, fight and flight were intimately intertwined, primal reflexes honed by her abusive first husband. Despite his desire to rush to her, take her into his arms, calm and soothe her, Drake knew he needed to give her space.

"Stop treating me like I'm broken," she told him, hands raised in a defensive posture, despite the distance between them. "Do you have any idea how humiliating it is when you tell a fellow professional to leave me out of a case involving my own patients?"

He noted the plural, his gut twisting with the fear that Alina's baby was gone forever. Because what would that do to Hart? "I apologize," he said. "I don't think you're broken. It wasn't about you or—" He stumbled, a sudden rush of grief miring his words. "Or what happened."

Her face flushed. "What happened?" She flung his words back at him, knotted with pain. "It didn't happen only to me, Mickey." She pulled both fists to her breast as if guarding her heart. "It happened to us."

Drake couldn't hold back. He raced around the table, gathered her in his arms. She didn't resist, instead allowing him to support her weight, share his strength. "I know, I'm sorry. I shouldn't have said that—" His own tears ambushed him. "I'm scared," he confessed, his lips hovering over the top of her head, his breath stirring her hair. "Cassie, I'm terrified. I feel like, if you don't walk away from this, I might lose you, too." He pulled back only far enough so he could cradle her chin in his hand and raise her face so she'd meet his gaze. "I couldn't live with that—it would break me."

She frowned, but her anger had dissipated, her expression more concerned than furious. "If you ask me to walk away, abandon Alina and her baby, I will." With each word, she moved farther and farther away from him until finally he stood alone, arms empty at his sides. "But the man I love, the man I know, he'd never ask me."

In the silence that separated them, Drake realized she was right. He wasn't afraid for Hart. He was afraid for himself. How could he be such a selfish bastard? Hart was doing what she thought was right despite her pain—not because of it.

"What if..." He hesitated. "What if we can't find Alina's baby? What if he's lost forever?"

Now it was Hart who stepped forward, wrapping both her arms around one of his, resting her head against his shoulder. "Then we'll know we've done everything we can. It's my fault. I convinced Alina to testify, to try the DNA testing. Because of me, she was targeted. But I didn't kill her, I didn't take her baby, and I'm not responsible for those other victims. That doesn't mean I still don't have a duty to try. My patients deserve everything I have—just like your cases do."

"But..." He had no words, no argument. Just a sick feeling in his gut, a need to protect her, their world, their life from...well, from everything. From more pain, loss. From the monsters stalking the shadows. He ached to take Hart into the bright yellow sunshine of the haven they'd created for their lost baby and keep her there, safe, forever. Protected.

Protecting his own heart.

It wasn't Hart's grief that had driven his words to Lucy. It was his own. At least Hart allowed herself to feel something, but he'd remained numb, distant, focusing on her as he barricaded his own feelings. And now what was escaping from behind his crumbling wall of denial terrified him.

His body shaking, eyes blinded by tears, he felt his knees buckle. But Hart held him up, arms around him as she guided him to their bedroom. She cradled his head in her lap as he wept, and he realized she wasn't the one who was broken.

He was.

Chapter 11

AFTER THE OTHERS LEFT, Lucy retreated to her office in one of the mansion's turrets. Although tiny, all the windows made it feel twice as large, and it had quickly become one of her favorite places. She glanced at the clock. Almost five. Nick was picking Megan up from jujitsu, and if Lucy left now, she'd make it home about the same time they did.

Or she could watch Alina's interview—the more formal, forensic interview done after she'd left the hospital and the drugs were out of her system. According to the file Wash had sent her, it was almost two hours long.

As always, she was torn. There was a baby out there, somewhere. A serial rapist to catch. How could she go home and enjoy her family, knowing that? And yet, how could she neglect them for her job? After all, they had no evidence that the baby was in danger, and there was no way in hell, given that they were waiting on the information on the other victims, that she'd catch this actor tonight.

Her family deserved the best she could give them. So did the victims. It was a never-ending tug-of-war on her psyche, and every time she thought she'd found the perfect formula to create some balance in her life, another predator came along to destroy that fantasy.

But there was one quick item she could cross off the mental to-do list swarming her mind. Actually, make that two. She called Graham Hunt.

"Have you decided yet whether to move forward with the grand jury?" she asked.

"Still weighing our options. If I do, I'll shift the focus away from the trafficking operation now that we've lost our key witness."

Actually, they'd lost three key witnesses, including the two women Lucy had rescued and persuaded to testify, but obviously Hunt was more concerned with the money trail tying his big fish to the operation.

"Your guy, the guy more popular than Santa Claus—"

"I can't tell you more. Not at this stage."

"Just, our new case, it involves a serial rapist using a designer drug. Something about it makes me think of the trafficking operation—"

"Probably you're just frustrated. I mean, I was after this morning. I doubt it's our guy. But, if you want, happy to go over your case, see if there are any ties."

In other words, she'd show him her hand, but he got to keep his cards secret. As if she might compromise his case.

"Let me get into it more, see what comes up." She matched his vague tone. "Any word on the CPA? Could he have been targeted?"

"Not looking that way, but the autopsy is tomorrow afternoon." A woman's voice sounded in the background. "Gotta go." He hung up.

Lucy stared at her phone, more frustrated than ever—and more certain than ever that she was the only one who cared about getting justice for Fatima and Maria, her two trafficked victims. Maybe Hunt's investigator, Estanza, was wrong. Maybe there was a way Lucy could track them down, secure their testimony... She racked her brain, trying to think of a sympathetic contact at ICE.

A text pinged on her phone. Megan. Amid a flurry of emojis that seemed more chosen to add color than to convey any meaning, were the magic words: Tonioo. Movie night In?

Lucy texted back two thumbs-up, a smiley face, three slices of pizza, and just for added measure, YES! in all caps. Then she grabbed her laptop and bag and headed out. She'd made it to the top of the steps when she turned back and retrieved Hart's folder from her desk. She could work after Megan and Nick went to bed—or maybe even during the movie. Best of all worlds.

She'd just pulled into the garage of their renovated Victorian in the South Side Flats when Nick's Escape appeared behind her. Perfect timing. Megan jumped out of the passenger seat balancing two

Tonio's carryout boxes. She still wore her gi with her hard-won brown belt. "Veggie for Dad and the carnivore special for us," she announced, waltzing past Lucy and into the house. "Zeke, down!" she shouted as Nick approached and took Lucy's bag for her.

Lucy leaned into him, waiting for Megan to corral their rambunctious golden retriever, enjoying a few moments of serenity before entering the happy chaos of their home.

"How was your day?" she asked him.

He wrapped an arm around her, his fingers kneading her tight shoulder muscles. "Better than yours, I'm guessing. How was the grand jury?" He knew how anxious she got about testifying.

"Canceled. Two of my victims were deported, and our key witness was hit by a car on his way to the courthouse." When she thought of it that way, it seemed obvious Hunt's case had been sabotaged, but she knew that was most likely a fallacy, her brain searching for a logical explanation for random events.

At least that's what she told herself. But as she thought about Alina's case, she had that same chill that had overtaken her back at Beacon Falls. Could the same man be behind both? Or was she imagining connections that weren't real?

"Got a new case," she continued.

"How cold this time?" Nick knew that Beacon Falls dealt with cases going back decades. The oldest Lucy had successfully tackled was a family killed by racially motivated violence back in the 1950s.

"Not cold. It's that girl who killed herself jumping from the Hot Metal Bridge a few days ago. She had a baby before she died, and he's missing."

He pivoted to stand in front of her. "How do you even start searching for a baby? Especially around here where we have so many home births—I mean, wouldn't it be easy to bribe a midwife into forging a birth certificate? Or maybe a lawyer draws up fake adoption papers? A baby could so easily be lost in the shuffle of hundreds of newborns..." He paused, frowning. "That's why you're looking, right? The mom gave her baby away before she killed herself? Or... You're not saying she did it, she killed her own child?"

"Cops couldn't find any evidence of that." She was hedging, and he saw it, she knew. "The mom, she was the victim of a sexual assault that led to the pregnancy. She'd just turned nineteen."

They both glanced in the direction of the open door Megan had gone through. "Only a few years older than Megan," he said in a low tone. "That's why you're so upset."

"One of many reasons. This case..." She hesitated, searching for concrete, professional terms, but coming up empty. "I don't have a good feeling about this case."

"One thing I've learned all these years," he said as he took her hand, and they walked into the house. "Never doubt your gut."

They entered the large kitchen. Megan had laid out the pizza, extra toppings, plates, and napkins. Nick grabbed a napkin and the smaller veggie pizza, forgoing a plate, and went into the adjacent living room, while Lucy selected a large slice brimming with bacon, mushrooms, pepperoni, prosciutto, sausage, and black olives. As Lucy sat on the couch beside Nick, Megan galloped down the stairs, now dressed in leggings and a Manchester United shirt, followed by the dog and then the cat as she returned to the kitchen.

"Did you feed them?" Lucy called.

"Doing it now!" The sound of the dog's gobbling confirmed her words.

"What movie did you pick?" Lucy asked Nick.

"Not me. Megan." He fussed with the remote, fine-tuning the surround sound. Basically avoiding answering her question. Which made her all the more suspicious.

"Megan," she called into the kitchen.

Her daughter emerged, holding a large bowl of steaming popcorn in one hand and a plate with two slices of pizza in the other and looking entirely too innocent for a fourteen-year-old. "Yeah, Mom?"

"What movie are we watching?"

"Oh, it's for my school project." Like father, like daughter—masters at avoidance. Probably because they both knew they couldn't lie to Lucy and get away with it.

Megan settled onto the camelback sofa, placing the bowl within reach on the coffee table. Nick clicked the remote. Lucy stood—she'd forgotten a drink. "C'mon, Mom," Megan said. "It's starting."

The dramatic theme boomed around the room as

the opening credits rolled. Lucy reached past Nick to scoop the remote from the coffee table and hit pause.

"Mom—"

"*Chinatown*? Really? Your teacher assigned an R-rated movie about—" She cut herself short, mouthing the word incest to Nick.

"Rated-R like a gazillion years ago," Megan protested. "She's my sister, she's my daughter!" Megan rocked her head as if being slapped. Popcorn kernels flew from the bowl.

"You've seen it?" Lucy asked.

"Twice. Like years ago. But this time, I need to study it. It was based on real events, you know. And with the whole Colorado River and other water wars brewing out West now, it makes for a great template for my paper on political corruption."

Lucy blinked. It was, in a typical Megan way, pretty damned brilliant. She turned to her husband, the maybe-not-so-brilliant psychologist who should have known their daughter was watching movies way too mature for her—although, honestly, Megan had pretty much been born an adult. Her sophistication always startled Lucy, made her wonder where this self-assured, confident creature who seemed to intrinsically know and understand the ways of the world had come from. Definitely not from Lucy, who'd had to "fake it till she made it" to overcome her innate anxieties her entire life.

Nick merely shrugged.

"Face it, Mom," Megan continued, slipping the remote from Lucy's hand. Her tone was bored, as if they weren't even actually arguing—because Megan had already won. "I learn about a lot more worse things when I read about your cases in the paper. And I've been hearing about those like forever."

Megan clicked the remote, and the movie continued. Lucy stood, hovering over the two people she loved most in the world, but her thoughts were still with Alina, a girl barely older than Megan. Suddenly, she felt ambushed by tears. She spun on her heel and headed into the kitchen.

"Maybe not tonight," she heard Nick say.

By the time she'd gotten a glass of milk and returned to the living room, he'd queued up another movie, one they'd all seen so often that they could repeat the dialogue by heart.

Megan flounced on the couch as she made room for Lucy to sit between her and Nick—Lucy's favorite spot in the entire universe. "Okay, okay. *The Untouchables*. Again."

"C'mon," Nick said. "You love this movie. Face it, Kevin Costner reminds you of me, doesn't he?"

"Eliot Ness?" Megan scoffed. "Puh-lease, Dad. You're no Kevin Costner."

"No? Who's Eliot Ness? Your mom?"

"Eliot Ness is a clueless idiot and much too uptight. Mom's Sean Connery—the old guy who teaches Ness."

Lucy choked with laughter as she swallowed a bite of pizza. "Wait, are you saying I'm old?"

"No, you're smart. Like the way you taught Dad when you first met. You know, how he was this geeky grad student doing research on stress in FBI recruits but was actually clueless."

"Not clueless," Nick protested. "Just a little naïve."

"Yeah, until Mom took you on a live fire training exercise, showed you what stress really was."

"Not live fire," Lucy hastened to correct. "Only paintballs."

"Still stung," Nick grumbled. "And you kept shooting me, always popping up where I wasn't looking."

"Kinda the idea."

Megan leaned back, smiling as she tossed popcorn into her mouth. "You two are such romantics. I'll never have a first date that good."

"Long time before we need to talk about that, right?" Lucy said.

Megan only grinned and shrugged.

"So if I'm not Kevin Costner, then who am I?" Nick asked.

"Duh. You're the geeky accountant."

"Cool. He's the one who figures out how to get Al Capone. Using his brains, not a gun."

The movie's opening scenes filled the screen with familiar comfort. Until Lucy remembered: Both Sean Connery's character and the accountant were gunned down in the end. Betrayed by their own.

Chapter 12

Lucy arrived early at Beacon Falls the next morning, hoping to have time to review their other pending cases before diving back into Alina's. She was surprised to see a strange car parked in the front lot. An older white Impala—the kind of unmarked vehicle Pittsburgh Police Bureau detectives drove.

Curious to see if it was Drake returned without his wife, she headed straight to her team's workroom. She stopped in the doorway. The whiteboards that lined the far wall had been covered with photos attached facedown, while the table was piled high with a rainbow of colored folders. The Goldilocks who'd masterminded this takeover sat at Wash's computer, typing away, hitting each key so hard she practically bounced out of her chair.

"Hey, you must be Lucy," she said without looking up. She resembled Goldilocks as well—if Goldilocks were a maniacal high school cheerleader with a Glock holstered at her hip.

"Nice to meet you, Detective Carter." Lucy set

her bag down.

"Stefi. Everyone calls me Stefi." Carter flashed a grin over the monitor. "Just fine-tuning my PowerPoint."

Lucy felt the vibration of the elevator rising. "You might want to hurry. And move that chair back to where you got it."

"Yeah, there wasn't one here. But it's not a standing desk—"

Wash rolled through the door. "Because it's a sitting desk, and I come with my own chair."

Carter wasn't fazed at all. She threw Wash a smile that would have opened doors to any nightclub. "You have an awesome setup here. Thanks for sharing." Somehow she finished typing, slid the chair back around the table, and had a hand out for Wash to shake just as he moved to regain his spot at the head of the table. "Stefi Carter. Sex crimes, crimes against children, crimes against elderly, special victims, and, oh yeah, now also domestic violence."

Wash glanced at Lucy before shaking Carter's hand. "Er, just call me Wash. Tech analyst." She kept his hand, waiting, and he added, "Forensic genealogy, database search, basically whatever Lucy needs me to do."

"Awesome. Nice to meet you, Wash." Stefi moved down the table, distributing a selection of folders to Lucy, then Wash. "Copies are in the file marked MJBG, and there's a PowerPoint there as well," she told Wash, nodding to his computer.

"MJBG?" Lucy asked.

"Multijurisdictional bad guy." Carter bounced on her toes. Lucy half expected her to start to do jumping jacks, the energy radiating from her was so palpable. "Guess you guys in the FBI would call him an unsub."

No one actually used the abbreviation for unknown subject other than in reports or on bad TV shows, but Lucy didn't correct the younger detective. She riffled the colored folders. They were all very thin except for the top one, labeled Alina Dolya.

"Those are in order. To go with my PowerPoint." Carter almost leaped across the table, an arm outstretched as if that would stop Lucy from sneaking a peek.

"Color-coded?" Wash made it sound like a question, but from his smirk Lucy knew it was more of an observation about Carter. The detective probably hadn't noticed, but while she'd been chatting up Lucy, Wash had been working at his computer, examining all of her data, no doubt. "TK's going to love that." He glanced at the clock. It was six after nine. "Where is she, anyway?"

"And Dr. Hart?" Carter asked. "I thought she'd be here as well."

Lucy checked her phone for messages. Nothing. "Let's get started."

Carter hesitated, obviously reluctant to have her carefully crafted presentation open to interruptions. ADHD, OCD, plus a hint of underlying anxiety were Lucy's armchair diagnoses. Then the younger detective nodded, danced around the chairs between her and the door, and turned off the lights. "Slide one, please."

Wash complied, but before Carter could proceed, a woman's shadow fell across the projected image. Cassandra Hart, Lucy noted—making her wonder where TK was. This was late even for the chronically late Marine.

"Sorry," Hart said as she slid into her chair.

"Is Detective Drake coming?" Carter asked, sounding hopeful. Drake would have seniority over her. Maybe this elaborate presentation was all designed to impress him? Lucy wondered.

"No. He caught a case last night."

"Okay, then. I wanted to start with our three surviving victims," Carter began.

"Three?" Lucy asked. "I thought we had six victims. And with Alina that makes seven hits from the DEA database."

"Yes, I'll be getting to that—" Before Carter could continue, another woman appeared at the door. TK, at last.

"Rough morning," she murmured as she edged behind Hart to take a seat. "Keep going."

Carter seemed a bit frazzled by the interruptions, and Lucy began to feel sorry for the detective. Given the budget cuts and additional caseload her department faced, she probably wasn't used to working in a team environment—especially not a team as independent-minded as Lucy's.

"Go on, Detective Carter," Lucy said.

"Stefi, please," she replied automatically. She

paced beside the projected image that overlapped the data she'd filled the whiteboard with. Took a breath and began again. "Okay. I've gotten the basic details from all the jurisdictions. Four of the other five jurisdictions welcomed our assistance and have shared their full case files—such as they are. Two victims were found dead and are still unidentified. Two more have died since, counting Alina. Leaving us with three surviving victims." She nodded to Wash, and a new slide appeared with a timeline. "But first an overview of the chronology. There have been no new cases reported with this same designer drug since Alina's assault nine months ago."

Despite Carter's physical exuberance and energy, her voice faded into a monotone, reminding Lucy of why she'd banned PowerPoint presentations for her team at the FBI. With the lights out and no eye contact, it was far too easy to distance yourself from the case, miss important details in the deluge. She pushed back her seat and moved to the light switch, turning on the lights. Hart blinked. TK was slumped down, eyes barely open. And Carter looked like she might start crying.

"Given that Detective Carter has so thoughtfully collated everything, maybe we can move on—after all, with an infant's life at risk, we don't have much time." She nodded to Carter. "Thank you for organizing everything and being so thorough."

Carter nodded back, but still seemed abashed, which only annoyed Lucy even more. Until Lucy realized why—she'd been exactly like Carter when she was a rookie, eager to please, anxious to not miss a thing. "Good job," she told Carter, making sure to meet the younger detective's eyes.

Lucy moved to the whiteboard Carter had so carefully prepared. She'd drawn a timeline across the top. Alina's name and photo were at the far right, with more photos turned facedown at varying intervals going back almost three years. The largest gap was between the first two victims, who had been found together, then there was a cluster of four victims, so close their photos overlapped, another large gap, and finally, Alina.

"Why the time gap after the first two?" She rapped her knuckles against the whiteboard. "Then the other victims were only weeks apart. Then nothing until Alina. Our actor was escalating—so why the gaps? And nothing since Alina's attack nine months ago? Has he changed his methods? Is he now killing his victims instead of using the drug on them?"

Lucy felt like she was back at Quantico teaching New Agents in Training. Even her voice had dropped into professorial mode. She glanced at her audience. Carter was bobbing her head in a nod, pen poised to take notes. Wash was typing on his computer—probably creating a database, correlating the info Carter had given him. And TK simply looked bored. But it was Cassandra Hart who caught Lucy's attention. The ER doctor was riffling through the paper files Carter had provided, her frown deepening as she turned each page.

"We need to try to interview the survivors

ourselves," Hart said. "But I'm afraid, if what they reported here is true, it might not do us much good."

"Why not?" TK asked.

Carter looked to Lucy for permission, then answered. "Like Alina, they had no forensic evidence other than the drugs in their system. And, also like Alina, they suffered severe amnesia."

"More than amnesia of the assault," Hart corrected the detective. "From these reports, Alina was lucky. She only lost the last few weeks of her life before her assault. Two of these women suffered severe retrograde amnesia—similar to what we'd see in a traumatic brain injury. They forgot large swaths of their lives. And the other not only lost her past memories, she's unable to create new memories. Is so debilitated, she's totally incapacitated."

"Which one is that?" Lucy asked.

"The third victim, the one after that almost year-long gap. Judith Miller."

As everyone opened the corresponding file folder, Lucy turned over Judith's photo. It was a candid shot of a woman playing with a large dog. She was in her late thirties, red hair, freckles. No similarity to Alina, at least not physically. But something about her smile, the hope in her eyes, reminded Lucy of Alina.

"So we have a total of four out of seven victims already deceased," Wash summed up. "How did the others die?"

"Two found DOA, one suicide," TK answered, flipping a file closed, tone grim. "And then Alina makes four."

"The suicide was due to a heroin overdose," Carter confirmed. "Family's statement was she began using after her assault, which was eight months before her death."

"Let's start with the victims in chronological order," Lucy said. "Often, the first victims tell us the most about the actor."

"Our first two victims were the DOAs," Carter said. "Official causes of death were also overdose. Their tox screens showed opioids along with our mystery designer drug."

"They were found together," Lucy noted. "Time of death estimated to be the same as well."

"Think he tried for a twofer right out of the gate?" TK asked. "This guy has some set of balls on him."

"Or he was with one victim, and the other interrupted, forced his hand."

"They're the only ones with opioids in their tox screen immediately after the assault," Wash put in. "And they had higher levels of the designer drug."

"Maybe he wasn't sure how much it took to cause the amount of amnesia he needed?" Lucy asked. She tapped their third victim's photo. "Then he skipped the opioids, adjusted the drug dose for Judith Miller, but it was still too much, caused more brain damage than he'd intended?"

Hart nodded. "Could be. There's so many variables involved, it's hard to say."

"Is it worthwhile interviewing victims at all?"

TK asked. "During the time you worked with Alina, did she recover any of her memories?"

Hart considered the question. "Over time, Alina caught fragments, similar to PTSD flashbacks. Nothing concrete, but maybe, given more time—"

Lucy nodded. "Carter, set up interviews for tomorrow. It'd also be nice to visit the dump sites, get an idea of how our actor chose them. Was he intimately familiar with the locations, or were they simply convenient?"

Carter bounced in her seat, eager to get going. Lucy moved to the far end of the whiteboard where the two dead victims' photos overlapped, still face down.

"Our first two don't fit the pattern, other than the drugs," Carter said. "They were the only two who suffered significant physical trauma. The coroner's report made it sound as if they were tortured—like military or Mexican cartel-type torture—before they died."

TK flipped open her folders. "Water in their lungs, petechiae from repeated suffocation, dislocated joints from stress positions." She glanced up. "She's right. These injuries were methodical, not a frenzied rage. Someone wanted something from these women, more than the sexual assault."

"Maybe it's not the same man?" Hart asked. "I mean, in my experience, rapists don't de-escalate over time. Just the opposite. They usually show more rage and violence, lose impulse control."

Lucy agreed. She turned over the photos of the

two dead victims, labeled Jane Doe #1 and Jane Doe #2.

At first, she barely glanced at the photos, other than to assess the level of decomposition. They'd been found not long after death: There were only moderate signs of insect activity. Even so, the coroner had done a decent job prepping the bodies for the photos. Had cared enough to want the women identified, brought home to their families.

In fact... They looked familiar. Hard to say with their slack features and vacant stares, but she could swear... Lucy grabbed for the stack of folders, fumbling for the right two. It couldn't be. She was imagining things.

"When were they found?" she snapped.

"Three years ago," Carter supplied.

"No. When. Exactly. The date." Lucy found her answer in the shuffle of paperwork. Two months after her team busted the sex trafficking ring and rescued the women from the warehouse on the North Side. Less than a week after she'd last interviewed Fatima and Maria to prepare the paperwork they needed to obtain their U visas.

Her two missing witnesses. Not deported by ICE—never even given the chance to enjoy more than a few days of freedom.

Her stomach rebelled as she considered the ramifications. The Zapata cartel had been working with the sex trafficking ring. If anyone knew how to torture two women to send a message, it was the Zapatas. Had they infiltrated a federal agency, gotten corrupt agents to do their dirty work for them? Or maybe they'd disguised themselves as ICE agents to gain access to her witnesses.

They'd killed Fatima and Maria. That made sense, in the warped, sociopathic mind-set of traffickers. Women weren't human—they were objects to be sold, bartered, beaten, used, abused, then discarded like trash.

But why take Alina? Unless her baby's father had ties to the sex trafficking ring or the cartel? Maybe someone high up the food chain, powerful enough that his son mattered even if the baby's mother was considered disposable.

Whoever killed her two witnesses knew where Alina's baby was.

She had no proof, no law enforcement authority. Just her gut instinct clamoring that this was no coincidence. Lucy glanced at the two women's photos. She didn't see their decomposed bodies. Instead, she saw the light return to their eyes when she'd explained the U visa program, heard the courage in their voices as they'd agreed to testify, to take back their power over the horror that had befallen them.

Remembered their shy smiles when they'd embraced her before she'd left that day. Smiles not unlike Alina's hopeful expression in her photo.

It didn't matter that Lucy no longer carried a badge. She wasn't going to let more innocents die.

Chapter 13

Lucy paced the space in front of the whiteboard, considering the team's next steps. Had Hunt lied to her about her witnesses being deported? No, wait. It was the HSI guy, Estanza, who'd told them ICE had taken Fatima and Maria. Maybe Hunt didn't even know the truth?

Or maybe he simply hadn't trusted Lucy with the truth.

She blinked, and the women's faces blurred, came back into focus. "I think I know these two victims," she said, parsing her words carefully. If Hunt was going to continue his grand jury investigation, she didn't want to say anything that might hamper his case. Especially if the Zapata cartel was working for the powerful man at the heart of Hunt's RICO conspiracy. "Part of a case when I was with the FBI."

"Can you tell us who they are?" Carter asked when Lucy didn't continue.

Lucy turned to face them. TK was engrossed in her phone, a frown on her face. Hart and Wash appeared curious, and Carter was braced against the table, one hand fisted as if she could somehow pull the information out of Lucy.

"I need to be sure first. Let me talk to some people. You guys start with the others. I'll get back to you when I can." Lucy grabbed her bag, slid the stack of Carter's folders into it, and left the room. She jogged down the steps and out the front door, debating her options. Call Taylor and pull in a favor, see if he could sweet-talk ICE into giving them any information to confirm or deny if the agency was involved? Just go to Hunt and demand to be read in on his top-secret RICO case? Or track down Estanza and ask him why he lied?

None of them felt right. Before she reached her car, TK came running past. She didn't acknowledge Lucy at all, her phone pressed against her face. Lucy hesitated, car keys in hand, but then put them back into her pocket. TK had been acting strange all week— ducking out to take phone calls, belligerently confronting Hart yesterday about Alina's case. Lucy knew there was something wrong, had hoped it would work itself out, but clearly it hadn't. She sighed and turned down the path to the gatehouse where TK lived, courtesy of Valencia.

It was more like a cottage than a house, and it actually was located nowhere near the gates at the front of the estate, but rather was nestled back in the woods on the far side of the mansion. It was built of local stone. The roof had been updated to a forest-green steel, and there were climbing roses framing the arched door at the front. If Cinderella were a former Marine with PTSD, still transitioning to life back home and struggling to find her place among civilians, this was exactly the fairy-tale cottage she'd build.

Lucy walked up the flagstone path, passing TK's motorcycle parked in the adjacent carport. The door was wide open, TK still talking on her phone.

"Don't do anything stupid," she was saying, but her tone wasn't angry, more like anxious. "I'm on my way. Promise me." She paused, her back still to Lucy. "All right. I'll see you soon."

Lucy rapped her knuckles on the door to announce her presence, then stepped over the threshold into the cottage's main living area, which consisted of a fireplace, sofa and two overstuffed chairs, and an eat-in kitchen. As always, the place was immaculate, with no signs of its occupant's personal life. TK had created another barracks for herself, although more comfortable than any the Marines offered.

"What's wrong?" Lucy asked as soon as TK hung up. TK didn't turn to face her right away, instead opening a closet to grab a large military rucksack. "Is it this case? I know you haven't worked many sexual assaults—"

"No. I can handle the case." Pride edged TK's voice. "But I can't stay." She hugged the pack to her chest, slowly spinning around, her gaze taking in every inch of her home as if she might never return.

Lucy couldn't help but think of when she'd first met TK. She'd been living in the storeroom of the gym where she'd taught self-defense and parkour, fighting to treat her PTSD with sex, alcohol, and violence, unable to hold a job for more than a few weeks. But here, at Beacon Falls, she'd found her way forward, had started therapy at the VA, earned her PI license, had even opened herself up to a relationship—albeit a long-distance one.

"What happened?" Lucy asked. "Is it David?" TK's boyfriend was an investigative journalist, prone to sometimes taking his search for the truth too far. "You know, if he's in trouble, Valencia and I will—"

"David's fine." TK shook her head. "It's a friend. We served together. She—she had it rough." She cleared her throat. "Has it rough. Needs my help."

"Where is she?"

"Alabama. I'm hitting the road now."

"Alabama? That will take hours. Why not fly?"

"I'll need wheels, and the fastest flight I could find wouldn't get me there any sooner than my bike."

Lucy hated motorcycles and hated even more the idea of TK driving through the day and into the night on one, exhausted and worried. "Take one of Valencia's cars. She won't mind—in fact, she'll be more pissed off if you don't."

TK considered it. "I haven't told Valencia. Was hoping you would?" She sounded so much like Lucy's daughter at that moment that Lucy almost laughed. Instead, she hugged TK, a quick, easily deniable hug, as she knew TK was prickly about shows of sentimentality.

"I'll explain to Valencia if you take a car and

promise to call or text once you're there."

TK rolled her eyes. "Yes, Mom."

"Sure you don't want to talk about it? Or need any help?"

"Not my problem to talk about." She hesitated. "Let me see what's going on, but I might call you or Nick for advice, if that's okay."

"Of course. Anytime, you know that." Lucy turned to the door, knowing how difficult it was for TK to admit she might need help and not wanting to embarrass her. "Seriously, call if you need anything. And be careful."

"Always." TK's phone buzzed again. A sigh escaped her, and she turned away to answer. Lucy left her there, hoping the former Marine wasn't headed into trouble.

But she had her own problems to sort through. Starting with Graham Hunt and his RICO target.

CHAPTER 14

Cassie watched, surprised as Lucy grabbed her bag, and walked out without a glance back. "What's going on? We can't just quit—"

Wash and TK exchanged confused glances. "Hey," Wash said, a false grin on his face. "Looks like I'm Charlie and you guys are my angels."

TK's phone rang. She frowned and stood. "I have to go." She jogged out the door, following in Lucy's steps.

What the hell?

Cassie turned to Stefi, feeling awful about the way Lucy and her team had treated the detective. Sure, Stefi was a bit unorthodox, could rub people the wrong way, but she was committed to her cases and her victims. She didn't deserve to be dismissed so abruptly. "If Lucy is dealing with the first two victims, why don't you and I start with the last two, the ones right before Alina?"

Stefi straightened her folders, shuffled the two cases to the top, then squared off the corners of the pile once again. She didn't make eye contact, her shoulders slumped as she nodded.

"I'll send everything I can find on them to your phones," Wash promised. "And, Stefi, thanks to your groundwork, there's a lot here for me to work with. Thank you."

Stefi braced her palms against the table. "So that was the great Lucy Guardino. I was so honored when she called and asked for my help."

"You did help. Lucy's never like that, honest," Wash told her. "I don't know why she took off like that, but it had to be important."

"I'm taking time from my own cases. My victims are important, too."

"If we can find Alina's baby and stop this guy from striking again, it will be worth it," Cassie said.

That got a stiff nod of acknowledgment from Stefi.

"Detective Carter," Wash said in a contrite voice, using Stefi's rank as an apology as much as a sign of respect. "I was hoping—there's one area where you have access to information we can't legally obtain. Birth records."

Stefi nodded. "I already submitted a request for all recorded male births during the time frame. Problem is, since Alina could have given birth anytime, from weeks ago to the day she died, that's a huge number, even if we limit it to Allegheny County. And now that we have knowledge that our actor readily crosses county and even state lines—he could have registered a home birth almost anywhere."

"It wouldn't take much," Cassie said. "A bribe to a midwife or family doctor and the birth certificate could say anything he wanted."

"I thought as much," Wash said. "Just hoped maybe—" He straightened and smiled at both women. "No worries. We'll get this guy. We just need a bit more data. I'll keep working the info Stefi brought. You guys send me anything new you learn."

Cassie glanced at the whiteboard with the women's photos. Seven women who'd suffered like Alina. "You know, these women might just be the tip of the iceberg. How many more victims are out there?"

Stefi slid her folders into her attaché case and clicked the locks. "Focus on the ones we know about. That's the best we can do."

"I'll call you with anything Lucy finds," Wash promised as Cassie and Stefi left. Together, they walked out to Stefi's unmarked departmental car.

Stefi drove like Drake did, one wrist draped over the steering wheel, eyes in constant motion, searching for anything out of place. Cassie smiled at the thought of Drake and the former Miss Pennsylvania turned police detective having anything in common. But then Stefi's gaze landed on her.

"Do they know?" she asked. "About you and Alina?"

Cassie shifted in her seat. Away from the question, away from the truth. "They never asked. Hearing about a missing baby was enough to get them to take the case."

Stefi made a noise of disappointment that sounded suspiciously like Cassie's third-grade teacher at Our Lady of Sorrows. Sister Jude. Always pummeling her students to try harder and never satisfied with the result.

"You should tell them. They're going to find out sooner or later."

"Why? What does it matter? Especially now that we've discovered these other victims."

"They should know that Alina gave you her medical power of attorney and made you the guardian of her child if anything happened."

Cassie sat rigid, pretending that if she said nothing, maybe Stefi would drop it.

"I think maybe..." Stefi continued but in a softer tone. "Maybe knowing that you'd never give up on her baby, that even if she was gone, you'd find a way—maybe that gave her some comfort."

"Right," Cassie snapped. "Comfort. As she hurled herself off a bridge." She sniffed back a sudden barrage of sobs before they could overwhelm her. "It's not as if Drake and I need the distraction of a baby in our lives right now—or have the time and energy. It's not as if we planned any of this." Her voice became shrill, her words ricocheting off each other. "We didn't kidnap and rape Alina, kidnap her again, steal her baby, and force her to kill herself."

Cassie slumped against the seat, blood draining from her face, hands clasped over her belly.

"Why are you so defensive about it? Personally, I think it was the hand of God. I mean, you save Alina's life, but then after—after you lost—she kinda saved you, too. Right?" Her tone upticked, uncertain and confused. "I'm sorry. I just saw the way you were with her when she was so scared about her baby. You sorta saved her twice."

"She saved me," Cassie confessed. "After...I was numb, like I wasn't even in my own body anymore. But Alina..." She turned away, pretending to look out the window at the riot of autumn color. "You know, she was there. When it happened. We were at Target, shopping for baby stuff. I hadn't even told anyone, except Drake. I mean, I was already eleven weeks, but that old superstition about waiting to say... I guess maybe it's not a superstition after all. More like a way to hide."

"I'm so sorry. You know you don't have to hide. You can talk to me. If it helps."

"Thanks. I'm better now, at least doing okay. Drake, he was so strong at first, but now it's like it's finally catching up to him."

Stefi nodded. "Yeah, I figured when he asked me to try to keep you away from this case. As if. I was like, have you met your wife? And he was all grouchy alpha-wolf protective."

"Sounds like Drake."

"When we find the baby—" Stefi started. Cassie loved that about the detective. Despite working on some of the most horrific crimes, with the most traumatized victims, Stefi was a constant optimist. "I mean, are you and Drake going to—"

"Yes." The one syllable made Cassie feel

lightheaded—but in a good way. "Yes," she repeated her promise—to Alina, to herself, to the baby. "We'll adopt Alina's baby, care for it as our own."

Chapter 15

Lucy left TK talking to her friend in soft, calming tones on the other end of the phone line. Once she reached her car, she called Graham Hunt. "We need to talk. Are you free?"

"I'm at the pediatrician's—took the morning off. But we're checking out. I can meet you at my house in twenty minutes or so." He gave her an address on Kakakitty Lane, which despite its silly-sounding name, was in an exclusive section of the already upscale Fox Chapel neighborhood.

Morning rush hour traffic was past, and the back streets were fairly empty, so she arrived at Hunt's gated drive right on time. Someone must have been watching for Lucy, because the metal barrier slid open before she could press the buzzer. The drive wound through thick trees, as if she were entering a fairy-tale forest. Then the trees opened, revealing an English manor that could have been transplanted from an episode of Downton Abbey.

She parked the Subaru between a black Mercedes sedan—Hunt's, given the federal courthouse parking permit—and a gray Toyota RAV4 Hybrid and walked up the steps to the front door.

Lucy rang the doorbell, sonorous chimes echoing in the house beyond. A few moments later, it was opened not by Hunt, but by a woman in her late thirties carrying a baby. "You must be Lucy," she said, shifting the baby to offer a hand. "I'm Rebekah. It's so nice to finally meet you. Graham always said any case you brought to him was a surefire slam dunk with the grand jury."

Lucy shook Rebekah's hand, and they moved inside the graciously appointed foyer. There was nothing ostentatious about the decor. It was understated and elegant, which told Lucy it probably was also very expensive. What surprised her, though, was Rebekah Hunt, who despite having a newborn, appeared camera-ready and full of energy.

"I'm so sorry to disturb you at home," Lucy offered. "I didn't realize you had such a young baby."

Graham came bustling in from the rear of the house. "Two weeks yesterday. We just came from the pediatrician—ninety percentile across the board." He beamed with the pride of a new father, taking his place beside Rebekah. Together, they looked like the poster couple for an advertising campaign. Or a Neiman Marcus catalog.

Rebekah smiled, turning her baby so Lucy could see his face. He remained blissfully asleep, and despite the fact that Megan was fourteen, Lucy felt a pang of yearning for another one of her own.

"He's perfect in every way. Look, he even has his father's dimple and the cleft in his chin." Rebekah nuzzled the baby. "You may look just like your father, but you're all mine, aren't you?" Then she sniffed and chuckled. "Especially times like this when you need changing." She nodded to Lucy. "Nice to meet you, Lucy. I'll let you get on with your business."

Graham led Lucy into a room off the foyer. It was a library with floor-to-ceiling bookshelves brimming with volumes that actually appeared to have been read, given their worn bindings and the few broken spines Lucy glimpsed. "Congratulations," she said. "I didn't even know you were expecting a baby."

He shook his head. "This case, it's pretty much consumed me. Thank God for Bekah. She never complained one bit, not even about me not taking any leave."

"Motherhood suits her. I remember when Megan was that age—I'd go for days without sleeping...or showering. Rebekah looks—"

"Radiant," he said, staring past Lucy out the open door, as if hoping to see his wife reappear. "Glorious." Then he shifted his gaze back to Lucy. "Anyway, what can I do for you? You said you had news? About the case?"

She showed him the photos of the two dead women. "Look familiar?"

He pulled a pair of reading glasses from his shirt pocket and peered at the images. "I see a resemblance to our two witnesses. Maybe. Where did you get these?"

She explained about Alina and the related cases. Hunt glanced at the photos again. "You're saying you think ICE agents took these women and what? Killed them? And then listed the women as deported in the database so no one would look for them?" He handed the photos back, shaking his head. "I agree, it's a coincidence, two women so close in appearance to our witnesses, but without positive identification..." He trailed off. "I just don't see how it's even possible. It couldn't be the work of one or two rogue agents. There'd need to be supervisors and—"

"Just like there were supervisors and administrators involved in the human trafficking ring. And with the Zapata cartel's involvement as well... People are people, we all have our weak spots. Find the right vulnerabilities and men with money and power could own anyone."

His eyes narrowed at the mention of the cartel, so Lucy pressed the issue. "How well do you know Jared Estanza? Did he come to you with the information that Fatima and Maria had been deported? Did you ever see any documentation yourself?"

"You think Jared is the cartel's mole inside Homeland?" He shook his head. "He's got more reason than anyone to hate the cartel and the man using it as his private army. No. If there's a mole, it has to be someone else."

"And you still won't tell me who this man, your target, is? We have three women confirmed dead.

Lord knows how many more might be out there—not to mention the victims he's left alive."

She felt his hesitation, knew he was torn between resurrecting his case and the difficulty of investigating a federal agency. "Least you can do is verify their identities. The FBI has their fingerprints—they wouldn't be in AFIS since they were witnesses, so the local department wouldn't have been able to ID them on their own. A simple phone call. That's all I'm asking."

He shifted his weight, shoving both hands in his pockets, blew his breath out, then finally gave a nod. "Come with me. There's something you need to see."

Puzzled, Lucy clutched her bag with the case files to her side—mostly so she wouldn't accidentally knock over any of the beautiful and above-her-pay-grade sculptures and vases that lined the hallway he led her down. They moved into the rear of the house, past a formal dining room, a room that was probably called a sitting room, given its abundance of settees and overstuffed chairs, then took a turn leading them away from a spacious kitchen sparkling with chrome and polished marble, through a hallway with windows on both sides, into a separate wing.

He finally paused before a large oak door, his hand resting on the knob. "I couldn't tell you anything before, nothing was actionable, but maybe now—"

With that inscrutable statement, he opened the door and ushered Lucy into a large rec room that had been converted into a command center. Whiteboards and corkboards filled the walls, littered with photos, reports, and scrawled arrows and questions. Two large tables sat in the center, piled high with papers. At one of them, Jared Estanza, the Homeland Security investigator, was working on a laptop. He glanced up, a question in his eyes when he saw Hunt with Lucy.

"She has new information," Hunt explained. "Tell him about your case."

Lucy told them about Alina, ending with the video Wash had found of the day she was kidnapped.

"That's me," Estanza said when she froze the recording on the image of the man texting. She continued the video. "And there's Graham."

"We must have been meeting the DA about a case," Hunt supplied. "No idea which one. It was so long ago."

Lucy rewound the video clip. "And that shadow is Alina right before she was grabbed by two men in ICE jackets. She was never heard from again. Five days ago, she jumped off the Hot Metal Bridge."

"Naked girl? From the news? That's her?" Hunt asked.

"Why did ICE detain her?" Estanza asked, already sounding defensive about his brothers in black.

"They have no record of detaining her. She just vanished for almost three months."

"But in that picture, she's pregnant. What happened to the baby?" Hunt glanced at the door, thinking about his own son, no doubt. Lucy had seen the same expression on Nick's face after Megan was born, wary and fierce, ready to protect his daughter against any threat.

"We think the actor held Alina prisoner long enough for her to have her baby, then somehow convinced her she should kill herself—maybe he threatened the baby if she didn't—while he kept the baby."

Hunt appeared shocked, but Estanza approached Lucy's theory with the skepticism of a lawman. "You think? Any evidence? And how does this tie to our case? One girl raped and kidnapped, a tragedy, yes, but hardly a federal case."

"Not one girl," Lucy answered. "So far, we've found seven victims."

"We were right there," Hunt murmured, taking Lucy's phone and rewinding the video. "We were both right there. They took that girl right in front of us—right in front of everyone—and nobody did a damned thing about it."

"ICE uses courthouses as easy targets," Estanza reminded him. "We had no reason not to think it was legit."

"Seven victims?" Hunt asked, finally catching up to the conversation. "Including our two missing witnesses from the trafficking case."

Lucy handed Estanza her case files, opening to the photos of their dead Jane Does. "Looks like. We need to verify their IDs. But I'm certain. It's Fatima and Maria."

"You don't think these are men pretending to be agents?" Estanza asked as he glanced at the photos.

"I think they were ICE, paid to make certain

witnesses disappear." Lucy straightened her shoulders.

"That bastard went after my witnesses." Hunt sounded aggrieved as he paced the space between the tables. He stopped, turned to Estanza. "It was him. Had to be."

Lucy dropped her bag onto the closest table, letting it hit with a bang that grabbed the attention of both men. "It's time you gave me a name."

They exchanged glances, Estanza shaking his head. Clearly, he didn't trust Lucy—fine with her, she didn't trust him either. Finally, Hunt met Lucy's gaze. "You're not going to believe me."

"Right, your evil Santa Claus. But if you can't convince me, how are you ever going to convince a jury?"

Hunt hauled in a breath, exhaled slowly. Then he straightened, shoulders back, as if meeting a challenge. "Marcus Gold."

Lucy fought to keep her surprise from her face. Marcus Gold was biotech's equivalent of Steve Jobs or Elon Musk. He traveled the globe, stopping pandemics with new drugs. He was leading the fight against climate change with his genetically modified bacteria that could digest plastics and other landfill waste to produce water, oxygen, or energy. And his experimental stem-cell treatments were designed to help patients with spinal cord injuries to walk again. Dozens of humanitarian groups had him on their boards of directors. He'd been nominated for a Nobel—twice—and was more popular than any politician or Hollywood star in the past decade.

"Marcus Gold?" she echoed.

Hunt responded by turning around one of the whiteboards. A hierarchy pyramid revealed the players in not only the sex trafficking network, but several other criminal enterprises. And at the top, over all of them: Marcus Gold.

"You're sure?" she asked, taking a closer look at the evidence mapped out on the various boards surrounding her. "Why? He's already richer than God. Why risk everything, get his hands dirty?"

He scoffed. "The risk is why. He's a charismatic psychopath—gets off on pushing the edge a little farther each time. Loves taunting us, and if what you say is true, he's now even getting hands-on with victims. Although, honestly, how much of a risk is it, really? With his money and power, who's ever going to suspect him, much less successfully build a case against him?"

"We are," Estanza put in, his tone grim. "We're going to stop him."

"Why?" Lucy asked, sensing a personal motive behind Estanza's vehemence. "Beyond the fact that federal agents may be acting as Gold's personal enforcement squad." If Gold was actually their man, she reminded herself. She'd want to examine all the evidence herself before being sold.

Estanza looked away for a moment, then turned to glare at Gold's headshot at the top of the power pyramid. "He had my squad killed—almost killed me as well. A few years ago, down in Texas. We thought we were tracking a Zapata cartel coyote, but it turned out to be much more than that. We walked into an ambush—set up by our own people."

He fell silent, lips clamped together, clearly not ready to share more details. Lucy turned to Hunt. "And you? You're getting ready to run for the Senate. Why risk everything by going after one of the richest and most powerful men in the world?"

Hunt nodded as if giving himself permission to answer. "Because I've known Marcus Gold for over two decades. We went to school together. God help me, I helped him become what he is today."

Chapter 16

LUCY STARED AT THE US ATTORNEY, suddenly uncertain that she could trust him at all. She walked around the perimeter of the large room, trying to compose herself. On the walls was evidence of several investigations, many centered around smuggling operations—Estanza's contribution, since his job was to investigate corrupt ICE and CBP agents. Maybe he'd be the voice of reason.

"You're conducting an off-the-books investigation into Customs agents you think are working for Marcus Gold."

"It's not off the books," he snapped, obviously aware at how closely he was skimming the rules. "Inspector General investigators are independent. We can choose to follow evidence where it leads us, work outside the usual chain of command."

"In the rec room of a prosecutor who's admitted that not only is he biased, but might also eventually be called as a witness? Not to mention your own admitted conflict of interest?" Lucy didn't intend to allow her frustration to bleed into her words, but dammit, they were professionals. Didn't they see that any case they built could never be prosecuted? They'd doomed their case—and maybe any chance of seeing justice for Alina and the other women—before they'd even begun.

"I gave Estanza my statement before he began," Hunt argued, using his courtroom voice. "I'm acting as a cooperating witness, not a prosecutor."

"But you are the prosecutor on the sex trafficking case. Why didn't you recuse yourself once you realized your old friend was involved? Maybe it would have saved Fatima's and Maria's lives." Not to mention the accountant who was killed yesterday. Suddenly, that didn't seem like an accident at all.

"I'm sorry. I had no idea about the women. But they're all the more reason to nail any corruption in ICE—if we find the agents involved, we can build a case against Marcus."

"Right." Lucy backed up, making sure the exit was behind her and both men were in front. The room was filled with possible investigatory leads, but so far she'd seen no evidence directly implicating Marcus Gold.

"I know it sounds insane," Hunt told her. "But you don't know the real Marcus Gold. I do. It all began at the Goode Academy."

"The private college in Sewickley?" The school had been founded almost two centuries ago by Pittsburgh's most prestigious families. Its alumni included the Carnegies, Mellons, Heinzes, and yes, the

Hunts.

"The men we linked to the sex trafficking ring, they all attended," Estanza told her. "But they're just the tip of the iceberg."

"They were all members of a secret society, along with Marcus Gold," Hunt added.

"So our criminal enterprise is really just a college fraternity?" Were they both delusional? How much of their so-called evidence was even real? Maybe it was all twisted to suit their paranoid fantasy, their need for retribution. Estanza had lost his team— she could understand guilt driving a vendetta—but what was Hunt's excuse?

"The Goode Fellowes society began that way," Hunt said. "A gentleman's fraternity, brothers for life. Generations of business and social partnerships forged between its members. It began as a social club, with introductions to the proper mentors, endorsements to ensure the right men were elected to public office, a little insider trading here and there. But then things changed. The academy began to allow scholarship students—brilliant minds who might not have come from money but whose inventions and ideas could pave the way to riches for those smart enough to partner with them. Marcus was one of those scholarship students. But he wasn't content with the free education, the guaranteed funding for his endeavors. He was desperate to join the academy's elite, the Goode Fellowes society."

"Wait," Lucy interrupted him. "How do you know all this? Were you a member, too? With Gold?"

Hunt's tone turned bitter. "Yes. Marcus destroyed the Goode Fellowes. Corrupted it. Do you know how he got in? He hacked the school security system, installed his own cameras and microphones— blackmailed us. Not just us. He threatened our parents, everything they'd built, our families, our legacies. He could have destroyed us. So we gave in. We thought, what harm could it do? After all, he's brilliant, his ideas could help us, preserve our families, build our futures." He made a sound that was half scoffing laughter and half strangled curse. "We were idiots. For decades, Marcus has been using the resources of the Goode Fellowes to not just make him billions of dollars, but to build a network that makes him untouchable."

"Why go after him now? You said he's been doing this for years." Lucy asked. She couldn't help but wonder if Gold had anything to do with Hunt's own career prospects.

"Because he's gotten cocky, reckless. He's gotten a taste for violence, and he likes it."

"You mean that Marcus Gold is personally involved—" It was so absurd she couldn't even finish the thought.

"It was him," Estanza said. He stood in front of the photos of his dead teammates, as if protecting them, hands raised in a defensive posture. "Gold watched as the Zapatas mowed down my team. If I hadn't been providing overwatch, away from the action, I would be dead as well."

That connection even further doomed their case,

Lucy didn't bother to point out. It was clear both men were obsessed, blind to the fact that their personal involvement had compromised any case they could build. She turned to Hunt. "And besides being your frat brother, what has Marcus Gold done to you?"

Hunt glanced past her out the open door, back to the main house. "He's threatened my family. Told me if I didn't stop the sex trafficking case, he'd kill them."

"And he got what he wanted, didn't he?"

"Not from me! I had no idea those two witnesses were dead—and I still built a case despite being told they'd been deported. I thought, this time, finally, I can nail him—"

"This time? You've tried to build a case against him before?"

"Yes. The first time was a few years ago. I thought I had him for money laundering, fraud, and extortion. But I never even had the chance to bring it to the grand jury."

"Tell her why," Estanza said in a low voice.

Lucy waited.

"I never brought the case because Rebekah and I were almost killed. Our car was slammed by a semi. I had to have my spleen removed. And Rebekah—" He choked, swallowed. "Rebekah lost the baby she was carrying. Our baby. She was in a wheelchair for almost a year before she was able to walk again."

His face twisted with pain, and he stepped toward Lucy. "That's the kind of man we're dealing with here. Marcus Gold is rich, powerful, and ruthless.

He'll do whatever it takes to win—because everything is just a game to him. We're not people, we're all just pawns."

Chapter 17

IN THE END, Lucy left Hunt's home after sharing only the specifics of the case involving Fatima, Maria, and Alina with him and Estanza. A simple fingerprint check wouldn't hurt her case and might give two families closure. But she wasn't about to risk the lives of any of their surviving victims. After all, who was to say that, given how the sex trafficking case had fallen apart, either Hunt or Estanza weren't working for Marcus Gold? Maybe their so-called investigation was merely a smoke screen aimed at rooting out any real evidence against Gold and destroying it?

If she believed any of the story they'd spun. They had a ton of theories and suppositions, but few facts to back them up. An elite college fostering a global criminal enterprise led by one of the century's greatest scientific minds? A billionaire philanthropist raping women, then wiping their memories? It was the plot of a bad thriller movie. She could almost see Nicolas Cage playing Marcus Gold.

As she drove past the expensive Fox Chapel mansions, she couldn't help but feel frustrated by both Hunt and Estanza. And angry—she was used to building cases fact by fact, not having them force-fed to her like predigested baby food. The two men obviously were blind to the fact that their personal involvement had hopelessly tainted any evidence they might find. Leaving her hands tied. She couldn't trust them. But...that didn't mean she didn't maybe believe them.

The way their rock-solid case against the men behind the sex trafficking ring had suddenly imploded. The carefully orchestrated kidnapping of Alina—in broad daylight, in front of a courthouse filled with law enforcement. A slap in the face, as demeaning as it was infuriating. Implying that there were men who lived beyond the reach of justice. And innocent women and children who paid the price, their own lives worthless, meaningless.

Not to Lucy. She gripped the steering wheel tighter as she followed the curving road leading her back to the highway. She took a few minutes to breathe deep—what Nick called tactical breathing, but she knew was actually a technique borrowed from mindfulness meditation. He was smart enough to know his clients would reject any hint of mumbo-jumbo unless it was couched in terms of gaining a battlefield advantage.

Then she called Mickey Drake.

"Something wrong?" he answered. She had to smile—that was the same way she responded to interruptions when she was immersed in a case.

"Hart said you caught a case. Any chance it was a pedestrian hit by a car yesterday morning on Forbes Avenue?"

"Nope. Mine was an ambulance hijacking gone wrong. Just nailed the assholes. Caught everything on CCTV, tracked them to the alley where they were shooting up. Idiots nearly OD'd. I'm in the ER now." He paused. "Pedestrian? That will be Jo Anderson over at Traffic. She's good, very thorough. Why? Something hinky about it?"

"I'm starting to think so. Victim was an accountant on his way to testify for the federal grand jury. Any chance we could check into it?" She used the pronoun in a vague fashion, knowing how overworked the detectives were—but also understanding the power of curiosity.

"Let me give Jo a call. I'll get back to you."

She gave him the accountant's details. "Thanks." She hung up, still feeling frustrated and uncertain. Should she tell the others back at Beacon Falls about Hunt's theory that Marcus Gold was involved in their case? If so, did he have Alina's baby? The man owned houses around the world, private jets, could pass through Customs without question—the baby could be anywhere.

The billionaire's rags-to-riches story was well known. He'd grown up south of Pittsburgh, in a village outside of Clairton, a perpetually impoverished coal town along the Monongahela River, south of Beacon Falls. She thought about that for a moment, then pulled into a Sheetz so she could safely use her phone. According to that always-useful yet always-questionable source, Wikipedia, Gold's hometown was Finely, Pennsylvania. Population 437, median income hovering just above poverty level, sixty-three percent of households led by single women with children.

Finely, Pennsylvania. She pulled out the color-coded file folders Carter had so carefully organized in order of the color spectrum, red through violet, newest to oldest. The folder for Judith Miller, victim number three, was robin's-egg blue. Lucy opened her file. According to the police report, Judith had been taken from her own driveway while leaving for work, was missing for four days before she'd been found naked, dumped behind a rest stop outside of Ansted, West Virginia.

Once they realized that the kidnapping had taken place in her hometown, and the West Virginia police found no evidence, the local police took over the investigation. In Finely, Pennsylvania.

Lucy sat back, the traffic coming and going from the convenience store barely registering. What the hell was a village with only four hundred people doing with their own police department? Most smaller towns couldn't afford the personnel, insurance, training, equipment, and other resources required to maintain a police department. Sometimes, they hired a few part-time officers to address municipal concerns during daylight hours and farmed out 911 calls to the State Police. Often, they simply relegated all law enforcement to the Staties, since in Pennsylvania most county sheriffs did nothing except serve papers and run the local jails and courthouses.

Finely was only half an hour south of Beacon Falls. And suddenly Lucy was in the mood for a trip out to the country. She called Wash to let him know she was headed out to interview Judith Miller, grabbed a handful of protein bars at Sheetz, treated herself to a pack of peach licorice, and headed toward Finely.

Driving along the gentle hills and farmland, she couldn't help but notice that the economic recovery that had graced Pittsburgh and its suburbs wasn't evident here. Many of the non-Amish family farms had For Sale signs posted along their fences. Abandoned homes littered the countryside, and the few that appeared to be occupied were in disrepair. It reminded her of when she was young, after her dad died and the Rolling Rock plant closed. Her mom had taken two full-time, albeit minimum-wage jobs just to pay the leftover hospital bills and keep a roof over their heads. As a kid, Lucy had resented her mom for never being there for her—but once she was older, she'd realized how lucky she'd been to have a mom willing to work so hard so that Lucy wouldn't be faced with the twin traumas of losing her dad and her home.

The minimum wage hadn't risen very much since then, not to mention covering other benefits like health care. And self-employed farmers? Amazing that there were any still left.

She passed through Clairton with its soot-stained buildings, caught a glimpse of the river, then turned inland, traveling through state forests and past more farmland until she began to see signs—large, colorful billboards, in fact—for the Finely Hunt Club. An oasis of hunting, shooting, fishing, and world-class accommodations, the signs proclaimed. One had a photo of a famous chef cooking a large, fresh-caught trout, with the proud angler looking on. Another showed a massive log cabin lodge surrounded by smaller private chalets. And the final one showed a beaming family emerging from a Cadillac Escalade brimming with luggage, obviously thrilled to have arrived at their vacation destination. At the bottom of each ad, she spied the words A Marcus Gold Property.

Giving back to the community, providing jobs and a tax base? Maybe Gold's endeavors were enough to fund public services like the police department. If so, Finely was lucky to have such a generous local son who hadn't forgotten his origins.

The signs to the Hunt Club directed her to turn down Gun Club Road, a newly paved two-lane street. At the intersection was a brand-new gas station and mini-mart. But Lucy didn't make the turn, continuing into Finely proper instead. Despite the expanse of empty land surrounding the town, the houses here were crowded together, most of them the uniquely Pennsylvanian elongated single-story frame houses with shingle siding and peaked roofs where poorly insulated attics would be turned into low-ceilinged bedrooms. She'd been inside so many houses exactly like this that she knew the layout by heart: The front door opened onto a living room/dining room, kitchen at back, then along the other side of the house would be bedroom-bath-bedroom with a narrow staircase up to the attic chiseled into the compact floor plan. No real hallways, and everyone could hear everything, the only privacy behind closed doors, or maybe down in the cellar with its stone walls and dirt-packed floor.

The roads here didn't show up on her nav system, but after she crossed the railroad tracks, she spotted the sign she was looking for: Pumpkin Patch Road. She turned down it, passed four houses shouldered so close together you could have borrowed a cup of sugar from your neighbor by leaning out a window, then there was an abandoned lot filled with debris from a burned-out house, followed by a weed-filled lot surrounded by a chain link fence containing a dilapidated frame house whose porch roof drooped so low Lucy doubted anyone could use the front door. Next to it was a spacious lot with a brick ranch surrounded by mature trees and a well-tended yard. Judith Miller's childhood home.

Lucy hadn't called ahead, but given Carter's description of Miller's disabilities, she figured someone would be home tending to Miller. And some things were best presented in person, face-to-face.

She took her time getting out of the Subaru, allowing anyone inside a chance to tidy up. There was a chain for a dog and a water bowl on the front porch, but she didn't hear a dog barking, announcing her arrival, so she gently tapped the doorbell like a proper guest and waited.

A few moments later, the door was opened by a

woman in her sixties or seventies, given her silver hair and the age spots covering her arms. She was trim, almost muscular, and wore jeans and a Steelers T-shirt that was a size too large. "Yes?"

Lucy held up her ID, a small billfold that held her retired FBI credentials on one side and her Beacon Falls business card on the other. "Ma'am, are you related to Miss Judith Miller? I have some news about her case, if she's available." She kept her tone polite. None of the victims or their families were under any obligation to cooperate, but she hoped that concern for justice, combined with curiosity, might persuade the Millers to at least have a conversation.

"I'm Bernice, Judi's mother." She scrutinized Lucy's credentials and returned them to her. "Judi's always available, but it won't do you much good. Come on in." She gestured for Lucy to enter.

The foyer opened into a living room where a thin woman sat in the corner of a plaid couch, staring out the bay window. There was a TV on beside her, featuring a nature documentary, but she didn't turn to face it or to look at Lucy. She wore gray sweatpants and a gray T-shirt, and her skin was sallow from lack of sunlight. Her face had no wrinkles, totally slack and expressionless, which, combined with her petite frame, made her look like a young child.

But this was no child, Lucy knew. Judith Miller had been thirty-six when she'd been attacked two years ago. She was the oldest of their victims. All the others ranged from their late teens to early thirties when they'd been kidnapped. What had drawn the attacker to Judith? Lucy wondered as she tried to picture the woman Judith had once been.

Bernice didn't do more than glance in her daughter's direction. "Coffee all right?" she asked as she led the way to the kitchen in the rear of the house. "Or I have tea bags. Not sure what kind, it's just for guests." Her tone made it sound as if it'd been a long, long time since the Miller house had hosted any guests.

"I'd love coffee," Lucy told her. "Just black, please." She looked around. The kitchen was bare-bones—original pine cabinets, old-fashioned countertops in a shade of yellow-green that had never been seen in nature, simple square table and chairs. But the place was spotless. She noted a row of baby bottles in the dish drainer and wondered if Judith could even feed herself. There was no masculine presence to be felt at all. The house felt hollow, as if the life had been drained from it.

Lucy joined Bernice as she poured coffee from an ancient Mr. Coffee, the white plastic stained to burnt umber from repeated use. Gingham curtains framed the window over the sink, revealing a spacious backyard with an old swing set and a large garden. At the rear of the property was forest, and to the side was the neighbor's chain link fence, weeds crowding through it.

"What a lovely view with all those trees," Lucy said. Bernice handed her a mug of steaming coffee, and they stood together at the sink.

"I raised three kids here—they're all gone,

moved to the city. Except Judith." She didn't sigh, simply took a breath as if she was long past sighing over her daughter's fate. "Lost my husband six years ago, figured it'd just be me playing granny. You know, Thanksgivings and Easters. Never figured—" A baby's shrill cry interrupted her. "Excuse me." She set down her mug and went down the hall, returning with a tiny baby, who was screaming his head off, his face wrinkled from the effort, limbs flailing.

"My granddaughter's," Bernice explained before Lucy could ask. With practiced hands, she spread out a small blanket over the table and lay the baby down. "She ran away last year with her so-called boyfriend. Then her dad calls me—she's at the hospital, overdosed, and pregnant, been living on the streets. Figure the best way to help her is to get her away from the city."

As the baby screamed, more shrill than the worst colicky cry Lucy had heard before, Bernice massaged his limbs, then bundled him tightly in the blanket. "She's clean and sober now, junior at Clairton High, but the baby, he was a premie, born addicted, so he's a handful."

"That's a lot for you to deal with, especially with Judith to care for as well."

She scooped the baby up. His screams hadn't eased. "Hardest part is you can't do any of the normal baby-loving stuff, not for this guy. He doesn't like eye contact or bouncing or singing or even touching, unless it's the special massage the therapist showed us. Makes it hard for his mom—she's just a kid, only seventeen—to understand how to love him. But," she moved past Lucy back out to the living room, "then we see how he is with Judith."

She approached the silent, still woman on the couch and held the screaming baby out to her as if an offering. Judith blinked, her gaze still fixed past Bernice, aimed vaguely out the window, and opened her hands. Bernice lay the baby in Judith's arms, and as she cradled him, rocking gently and humming, he grew still. He stopped crying and actually began to relax, his face transforming from anguished to contented.

"Makes you think God has a plan after all, don't it?" Bernice said as they stood watching the two on the couch. Then she turned back toward the kitchen. "They'll be fine for an hour or so, until the baby's next bottle is due."

She retrieved her coffee and sank into one of the chairs at the table, finally taking a good long look at Lucy. "So now. Former FBI agent. What can I do for you?"

CHAPTER 18

CASSIE AND STEFI DROVE to the home of the woman who was attacked before Alina was. Her name was Tandi Jefferson, and she lived near Harpers Ferry, West Virginia, but on the Maryland side of the Potomac. As Stefi reviewed the scant facts of Tandi's case, what struck Cassie most was the timing.

"I don't get it," she told Stefi. "He killed his first two victims together, then attacked four more, each only weeks apart, then nothing for several months until he went after Alina. Why did he stop?"

Stefi shrugged. "Could have been in prison. Could be other victims who haven't reported, so we have no idea they're out there. Could just be ordinary life stuff—even sadistic rapists have jobs and families to deal with."

"I don't think he was in prison," Cassie said. "He's so damned careful about not leaving any forensic evidence."

"Could've been picked up on a totally different charge. Stalking or harassment or trespassing—cops might have thought he was a burglar, not a sex offender."

"Maybe." Cassie scanned the file again. Like the others, it contained only the basic facts. Tandi was twenty-six at the time of her attack, was taken after leaving her gym, and was found four days later, naked and confused, in a strip mall's parking lot in Youngstown, Ohio.

She'd lost her job, but she either came from money or had negotiated a nice severance package, because the house they drove up to sat on prime real estate overlooking the river. The well-maintained Victorian was guarded by a state-of-the-art security system, requiring them to buzz in and show their IDs at the gate and again at the front door.

The woman who greeted them was thin but muscular and wore leggings, a T-shirt, and a wraparound sweater. She squinted at the sun as if she didn't make it outside the house much. As she waved them inside, Cassie noticed a stack of packages covering the dining room table, including a meal delivery service. Had her attack left Tandi Jefferson agoraphobic?

After she offered them coffee and tea, they settled into chairs in a glass-walled porch with a view of the river. Tandi curled up on her chair, legs tucked beneath her, taking a few breaths before answering each of Stefi's questions about what she remembered of the events leading up to the attack.

"I was doing pharmaceutical research and development—the drug used on me? It was my creation."

Cassie glanced first at Stefi and then back at Tandi. "You created the amnesia drug?"

"I designed it to help soldiers and people with PTSD, aid in their therapy." Tandi grimaced. "Before they stole it from me."

"Stole it? Besides you, who had access?" Stefi asked.

"Anyone in the lab. But don't bother. I know who did this to me."

That got their attention. "Who?" Cassie asked.

"The same man who stole my drug. Marcus Gold. It was his lab I was working in."

"Do you have any proof?" Although they were recording the interview, Stefi was furiously jotting notes in her notebook.

"I know it's him—before my attack, after he fired me and published my research under his name, I tried to sue him. But it's Marcus-freaking-Gold, so no lawyer would touch the case. I even went to the feds, tried to see if they could charge him with fraud or intellectual property theft, but they laughed me out of their office. Word must have gotten back to Marcus, because two weeks later he raped me. Used my own drug against me."

"Did you tell the police?" Stefi asked, riffling through her copy of Tandi's police report.

"I didn't know it was Marcus. Not at first. Took me awhile to figure it out and by then, I realized there was nothing the police could do. Not against Marcus. Nothing anyone can do."

"But why would he use that drug, knowing you'd eventually know it was him despite the memory loss?" Cassie asked. "If he's such an egomaniac, why not just show his face, knowing that without any evidence it'd turn into a she said/he said case, and you'd lose everything by going public?"

Tandi was shaking her head before Cassie could even finish the question. "No. No. You don't understand how his mind works. He wasn't just raping me, humiliating me—he was punishing me for daring to think my intellect was equal to his. Of course he used my own drug against me. To show me that there is nothing I can do that he can't take from me, that anything I create, he can steal and twist and pervert and make it his own. And the price of fighting him, of speaking up, isn't only physical injury, not only death, but losing the thing I value most—my mind. No. He knew exactly what he was doing, the twisted bastard."

Stefi exchanged glances with Cassie and then asked, "Can you remember anything? About the attack—he kept you for several days."

"No, it's all a blank. But a few months after, I started having dreams. Memories. Not of being raped, but later, at the end. I was naked, on the ground, and he stood over me, looming—like a monster in a horror movie. Then he leaned down and whispered in my ear, told me no one takes what is his. And I remember his tattoo."

"Can you describe it?"

"It's some college fraternity emblem. A snake with an apple in its mouth and its body forming the letter G. Marcus loves to roll up his sleeves, pretend to be just one of the guys. So I've seen it dozens of times before."

"Where is it?" Stefi had her pen poised over her notebook.

Tandi turned her left arm over and pointed to the inside of her wrist. "Here. Right here. About the size of a quarter."

"Did you only see it in your dream? Or did you actually see it during the attack?"

Tandi narrowed her eyes at the detective. "Look, I know you don't believe me, and even if you did, you aren't going to do anything. No one can. Not against a man like Marcus Gold. But I'm telling you the truth. Marcus Gold raped me. And he'll do it again."

An awkward silence filled the room.

"I'm afraid he might have already. Do you recognize any of these women?" Stefi arranged the photos of the other victims on the glass-topped coffee table.

Tandi leaned forward, her face expressionless except for a twitching in her eye. She shuffled through the photos, quickly rejecting the first three and Alina's, then pausing over the two women who'd been attacked before her. She picked them up and studied each one for several moments. Finally, she placed the photo of victim four, Marla Kitchens, faceup on the table.

"She worked in the stem-cell group—same research lab as me, different division. There was a rumor that she was dating Marcus and broke it off.

Then she was gone. I figured she quit, or he fired her." She tapped her lips with a manicured finger. "He didn't kill her, did he?"

"No," Stefi answered. "But she killed herself. A few months after her attack."

"Did he use my drug on her?"

Cassie nodded. "Yes. According to the police report, she lost almost a year of her memory."

Tandi nodded, her gaze fixed on the photo. "That's not how my drug was meant to work—he must have used a dose far higher than anything we tested." She glanced up at them. "My compound is meant to temporarily block the encoding of memories associated with strong emotion—just long enough to allow a patient to undergo a therapy session, overwrite the worrisome memories with a more neutral accounting of events. By combining such a massive overdose of the drug with an ongoing traumatic event—"

Her gaze drifted past them as she blinked rapidly. "The consequences could be devastating. Far worse than what I experienced—permanent cognitive damage." She shook herself. "I never realized that maybe I got off lucky."

"One of the early victims appears to be unable to form new memories and has regressed to early childhood," Cassie told her.

Tandi's expression went blank again. Then she released her grip on the photo of victim five, setting it on the table next to Marla's. "I don't know her name, but if you check the employee roster, I'm pretty sure she worked for one of Marcus' companies. I remember seeing her in one of his promotional videos—a real estate developer, maybe? Or maybe marketing? Definitely not in the science division."

"Thanks, we'll check into that," Stefi said, scribbling furiously in her notebook.

Tandi leaned back against the couch, her skin now almost as pale as the white leather. Even after she hit the back of the sofa, she kept pushing harder, as if trying to distance herself from the other victims. "That's all I know."

"Would you be willing to—"

"No," Tandi interrupted Stefi. "I'm done. It's not my fight anymore."

Cassie took the hint and stood. Stefi opened her mouth to ask another question, but Cassie touched her shoulder, and she shut it again. As Stefi gathered the photos and her files, Cassie stepped away from the couch, giving Tandi some breathing space. She understood all too well the claustrophobic, chest-crushing feeling that came from dissecting past trauma.

"Thanks," she told Tandi. "You've been a huge help."

Stefi placed a business card on the empty tabletop, centering it precisely. "Do you want to know if we make any progress?"

Tandi stood and moved past them to open the door. "Only if you nail the bastard," she finally said, looking past them to the vista beyond the front door. "That'd be worth celebrating."

Chapter 19

Lucy and Bernice returned to the kitchen. "After all this time, why are you here?" Bernice asked as she took her seat at the table. "Have you found the man who did this to my Judi?"

"No, ma'am." Lucy slid a chair out and sat down, folding her hands in front of her on the table. "But we have found other victims who were given the same drug as Judi. We're hoping to trace it back." She paused. "The others don't have amnesia as severe as what your daughter suffered. Some have even remembered bits of what happened."

Bernice shook her head. "Judi doesn't remember anything—what he did to her, that's gone, thank God. Only blessing that came from all this."

"How did the drug affect her?"

"It kinda—the word the doctor used—regressed her. Not just forgetting the events of her life but also more. She understands language, will sometimes even talk if she needs to, but she's a blank when it comes to how to act. Blank..." She took a sip of her coffee. "But not like a slate you can write on. More like...vanished. Erased. My Judi's gone, and she's never coming back. She'll need someone to care for her the rest of her life." Bernice set the mug back down, the sound echoing through the silent house.

"What's the last thing she does remember?"

"When she first came home, she kept asking for Bugsy—that was the dog we had when she was a little girl. He died when she was eleven. I had to cover all the mirrors because every time she looked at her reflection, she'd start screaming—seeing an adult woman instead of the little girl she expected to see. Then she just pretty much stopped talking altogether. Even after two years, she doesn't seem to understand she's any older. Like she's trapped inside her own memory."

Lucy took out the case files—Carter's organizational skills were coming in handy, she had to admit. "Do you recognize any of these women? Any chance Judith knew them?" she asked as she showed Bernice the photos of the other victims.

The older woman scrutinized them with care but shook her head. "No. Sorry. And I knew everyone Judi knew." A warning to Lucy not to even try to approach Judith. Bernice pushed back her chair. "The baby will be needing his feeding soon."

Lucy gathered her files and stood as well. They walked through the living room. Lucy paused, glancing at the collection of photos gathered on the fireplace mantel. The one front and center showed a laughing

Judith with a man, her hand held high, revealing a glistening engagement ring.

"Taken a week before—" Bernice said, her voice trailing off, one hand reaching to stroke the lost memory captured in the photo. "Michael hung on as long as he could—longer than most men, I guess—but time passed, and even he had to let her go."

Judith still had the baby nestled on her chest, neither making eye contact with anything, but both content.

"How old's the baby?" Lucy asked, thinking of Alina's missing infant. There was no way this boy could be Alina's. But Lucy couldn't help but wonder if Alina's child was being as lovingly cared for.

"He was a month early, so he's tiny. Almost two months now—and still hasn't smiled at anyone. The doctor says drug babies can be like that, that it takes time, but..." She sighed. "All we can do is the best we can." She opened the door and escorted Lucy out to the porch. They stood there for a moment, Bernice staring at the dilapidated property next door. "Can't help but think how different all this could have been."

"You mean if Judith hadn't been assaulted?"

"No. Even before." She jerked her chin at the neighboring house. "Hard to believe, but that's where Marcus Gold grew up. He's four years older than Judi, but as kids they were inseparable. He came home after college, after he'd made his first million, asked Judi to marry him. He was nineteen, she was only fifteen, had her own hopes and dreams. Was smart enough to know she didn't love him—not the same way he loved her. So she said no, not yet, give it time." She shook her head. "We thought she was so mature, handling it so well. But maybe, if she'd said yes..."

Marcus Gold. Marginally connected—possibly, if she could believe Jared Estanza—to their two dead victims, and now he'd also had a relationship with victim number three. Could he really have done this to a girl he once loved, not just destroyed her life but also erased her past and future? Or was he the target of some warped plan designed to implicate him? Either way, she needed to take a closer look at the billionaire genius.

Movement from the side window of Gold's old house caught her eye. "I think there's someone in there."

"Of course there is," Bernice said, turning away to rest her hand on her own door. "His mom still lives there. Never leaves—he has everything sent in for her."

"But the house is falling down. Surely it can't be safe."

"Way Felicia likes it, I suppose. I mean, not like he couldn't set her up in a fancy new place if she wanted." She opened her door and retreated over the threshold, obviously uncomfortable with discussing Gold's mother. "I have to fix the baby's bottle before he starts screaming again."

With that, Lucy was left alone on the porch. She started toward her car but couldn't help but stop halfway, staring at the Gold homestead. Who better to ask about Marcus Gold than his own mother? She eyed the tall chain link fence with its No Trespassing signs. There was a gate at the end of the drive. Nothing like Graham Hunt's imposing security barrier. Not even locked, it reminded her of gates on farms designed to keep livestock from wandering.

The gate opened with the creak of seldom-used hinges. Lucy approached the house. The way the porch roof had half collapsed blocked the front door. Why hadn't Gold gotten that fixed? Or maybe, as rich and famous as he was, he liked the idea of his mother's house appearing uninhabited from the outside? Camouflage to shield her from prying eyes? Although, a guy who was richer than God like Gold could afford the best security on the planet, so why even bother? But she couldn't think of any other reason, because even if Gold and his mother were estranged, a son—any son—would still ensure his parent lived in a safe space. Wouldn't he?

She walked around the far side of the house. There was no lawn, just dirt and the occasional jumble of weeds. As if, despite the forest surrounding them, nothing chose to live on this patch of land. The windows were blocked by dark curtains, so no light escaped from inside.

Rounding the corner, she scanned the rear of the house. There was a concrete slab porch, its steps cracked and pitted. A wrought-iron railing twisted around the edge of the slab and down the stairs. Lucy didn't touch the railing as she climbed, not trusting the rusted bolts that were meant to secure it to the crumbling concrete.

"Hello," she called once she reached the top. The wooden door had a window at the top and two windows on either side, all curtained. She tried again, raising her voice and knocking loudly on the door. "Mrs. Gold? Hello." She waited, not sure how long it might take an elderly woman to walk through the house.

There was a rustle of movement in the shadows beyond the nearest window. "Mrs. Gold, I'd like to ask you about your neighbor Judi Miller." Lucy figured the older woman would be tired of talking about her famous son, so she used a different approach. "I'm trying to find the man who hurt her."

The door opened a crack, too small for Lucy to see the woman who stood behind it. "Who hurt Judi?" Felicia Gold's voice whipped across the space between them. "I'll tell you who hurt Judi Miller. My godforsaken son, that's who."

Chapter 20

"Now say again who you are," Felicia Gold commanded from behind her half-open kitchen door. "Slowly. I'm recording everything."

"Yes, ma'am." Lucy suppressed a grin. Something about Felicia's tone of command reminded her of her own mother. She held up her credentials, keeping them at an angle so Felicia could read them without stepping forward. "My name is Lucy Guardino. I work for the Beacon Group. We investigate cold cases. We're partnering with the Pittsburgh Police Bureau to find the man who attacked Judith Miller."

"Judi wasn't attacked in Pittsburgh."

"No, ma'am. We've found several victims attacked by a man using the same drug that—" Lucy faltered, searching for the right word. "The drug that damaged Judith. We think the attacks are all tied together."

There was a lengthy silence. Lucy waited. Finally, the kitchen door swung wide. The interior of the house was in complete darkness. Felicia Gold wore jeans and a sweatshirt with an embroidered bluebird on it. She had long brown hair streaked with silver, pulled back into a braid. And her eyes were completely vacant.

"I'll tell you everything I know about Judith Miller on one condition," she said, standing defiantly in the doorway, her gaze skittering past Lucy.

"Ma'am?"

"First, you stop ma'aming me. Name's Felicia. Second, we get out of here, and you take me to DairyTreet for one of their footlongs and some soft serve. Then we eat it in the park near the river."

"That's three conditions."

"I'm blind, not stupid. Take it or leave it. I gotta get out of this house before I go stir crazy, and it feels like a nice day for a trip."

"I'll take it. Do we need to let anyone know you're going? Take any medicine with us?"

She harrumphed, stepping forward, closing the door behind her without locking it. "Medicine? I don't need no medicine—and don't you worry. What I got ain't catchin' none."

She held her arm out for Lucy to take. Lucy guided her down the dilapidated steps. "You live here alone? No one to look after you?"

"Like it that way. My son—the youngest of them, Marcus—he sends his spies around, keeps an eye on me, even though I tell him I just want to be left alone."

She pulled up short, turned to Lucy, fixing her with that eerie, vacant gaze. "You're not one of them, are you? Marcus didn't send you?"

"No. I really am here just to talk about Judith. You said Marcus hurt her?"

"Oh, that. That was a long, long time ago—way before she was attacked. Marcus has been in love with that girl since about the day she was born and he first laid eyes on her. Called her his pretty doll. We had to explain what a baby was after he wanted to take her home with him and picked her up, almost dropped her." She sighed. "My Marcus. Boy's got a genius IQ, two PhDs, more money than the Pope, and less common sense than God gave an earthworm."

They reached the gate. Lucy held it open with one hand and guided Felicia through it with the other. Then she helped the other woman into the Subaru.

"The DairyTreet?" she asked as she started the car.

"Yep. Best hot dogs around. I've been hankering for one for God knows how long. More than a decade, at least."

"A decade?"

"Been about that long since I've left the house for anything other than the doctor's. Marcus wanted me to move, but I can get around just fine in my house—lived there most of my life. I told him I'd never speak to him again if he ever forced me from it. So he said, 'Fine, stay here till you die.' And that's just fine with me, so we made a deal." She jerked her chin down hard. "Haven't spoken to him since."

"You haven't spoken to your son in over a decade?"

"Nope. Suits us both just fine."

"But—is it safe, you living there? The front porch is about collapsed, and those back steps—"

"Never use the front door, so that's no bother. I expect someone will be along to patch the back steps if they get much worse—that's what always happens. Something gets broken, or I have a doctor's checkup, or need groceries, and some stranger—Marcus' minions, I call them—will appear, get the job done."

Lucy thought about that. Felicia was right, Marcus Gold was spying on her, even though he refused to speak to her. What kind of man did that?

One used to getting his own way—without questioning or argument.

Felicia grinned, set her shoulders square. "He gets it from me. His stubbornness."

"What did you mean when you said he hurt Judi?"

"Oh, that. They were just kids—she was maybe fifteen. Marcus was all of nineteen, just graduated from college. Came home determined to make Judi marry him, go off with him to grad school, take care of him while he made his fortune. He knew even back then that he was going to be rich—said he'd buy her the world if she just said yes."

"What happened when she didn't want to marry him? That must have hurt him pretty badly."

"Thing about Marcus is, you think he has thick skin, like it all just bounces off him. Because he'll never show you anything, especially not pain. Not happiness, neither. But it's not true. Everything sinks in, so deep, it festers. When Judi said no, he went off to school like nothing happened. But then, a few years later, when she was up for a scholarship to college, she got arrested."

"Arrested? For what?"

"They found drugs in her car. Enough to be a felony. Everyone said they weren't hers, knew it, in fact. Judi never used drugs. Wanted to go to school, be a teacher. The judge threw the book at her—"

"Even though it was her first offense?"

"Yep. That's when we all knew Marcus had to be behind it. He never said a word, like she had it coming or something, just because she never loved him the way he loved her. Ruined her life." She turned to face Lucy. "I love all my children, dearly. I love Marcus. But that boy—" Felicia shook her head. "He doesn't understand pain. Not how to handle his own, not what it means to feel it in others."

"Empathy."

"Right. He doesn't have that. No idea why. He was loved, never even spanked as a boy. Maybe because his daddy died before he was old enough to remember him. I had my hands full, but we made do. I don't know what more I could have done differently. I just don't know."

"Felicia," Lucy gauged her words carefully, "do you think Marcus could ever hurt somebody? On purpose?"

"In business, money on the line, absolutely.

Growing up here, he always dreamed of more, more, more. No matter how rich he gets, it will never be enough."

"What about people? Physically?"

Felicia was silent for a long moment. "You mean like what happened to Judi Miller?" She clamped her lips tight as if holding her words back. But her chin bobbed in a nod before she finally said, "No. Marcus wouldn't do that to someone he once loved. No matter how much they hurt him."

What else could any mother say? Lucy noticed that Felicia didn't ask her why she might suspect Marcus—as if she already knew the answer.

As they drove, she spotted a police car in the rearview mirror. Lucy checked her speed—right at the limit. But the cop car's lights went on, accompanied by a burst of its siren. She eased onto the shoulder, expecting the car to pass on its way to an emergency, but then a second police car approached from the other direction, making a sharp turn in front of her, blocking the road.

She braked, hemmed in front and back.

"Why did you stop?" Felicia asked.

"I'm being pulled over by the police. I'm not sure why. I wasn't speeding."

"I know why. Because it's Finely. Marcus, he owns the town, owns the cops. He sent them." Felicia's chuckle was sharp and wry. "Damn him. I didn't even get to have my footlong."

Before Lucy could do more than put the car in park, the officer in the car in front of her was out of his vehicle, weapon aimed at her across the hood of his car. "Driver," came the amplified sound of a PA system from the car behind her. "Hands out the window. Now."

"Call Wash," Lucy told the car's Bluetooth assistant. As the phone dialed, she lowered her window and complied, moving with slow, exaggerated motions.

"Open the door," the officer commanded. Lucy did as she was ordered. The phone was ringing. "Exit the vehicle, keep your back to me, hands interlocked on your head." Lucy stood beside the car, now an easy target for the officer in front of her. "Good. Now back up. Slowly."

Lucy took one step, two steps, two more until she felt a man moving behind her—the second officer leaving his car. She reached the Subaru's rear bumper. "My name is Lucy Guardino. I'm a former federal agent."

"Quiet! Down, on your knees. Cross your feet."

She sank down into the mud and gravel and did as she was told. She had a flash of memory—performing similar exercises at Quantico, taking turns playing the bad guy. Except these two officers weren't highly trained FBI agents and were armed with more than simulated ammo. Her stomach clenched. She hadn't done anything wrong, there was no need to worry, her mind argued, but she couldn't make herself believe it.

Lucy heard Wash's voice as her call connected, but before she could answer, there was a rush of movement as the man behind her came forward, grabbing one wrist, then the other, quickly handcuffing her. His partner kept his gun trained on Lucy as he crossed the distance between them, telling Felicia to stay in the car.

"Officer, I'm former FBI. I'm carrying—" The man behind her shoved her head down to the ground, knee against the small of her back, cutting off her words.

She heard him reholster his weapon, then he used both hands to search her, yanking her Beretta and its holster from her waistband. Gravel bit against her face, and it was hard to breathe, much less try to explain. Lucy focused on her breathing, waiting for the officer to finish. He slipped her knife from her front pocket, stumbled a bit when he encountered the brace protecting her injured ankle but yanked the Velcro open and tore it off with enough force that pain twanged through the still-raw nerves. Then he slid his hands beneath her body, pressing against her intimately as he completed his search.

Finally, he slid her credentials free. She waited, barely holding her face up from the mud, assuming that as soon as he examined them, saw her concealed-carry permit, that he'd release her and they'd talk, clear up whatever confusion had led to the traffic stop in the first place. Yeah, they'd taken a highly aggressive approach, but she understood the need for officer safety, and obviously this was all a misunderstanding.

Instead, he said nothing, merely nodded to his

partner, who reached into the Subaru and came out with Lucy's bag, phone, and keys. Another car pulled up beside them—a black Town Car. A man emerged—dressed to match the car, complete with opaque sunglasses—and strode around to the Subaru's passenger side, where he opened the door. "Mrs. Gold? Let's get you back home now."

As Lucy craned her neck to watch, he helped Felicia out of the car and walked her over to the Town Car. Felicia turned, her empty gaze scanning the area. "Sorry, Lucy. My son..." She shrugged. "He always wins."

The man got her situated, and the car sped off. "You can release me now," Lucy told the man behind her. He said nothing. "Look, I get it. You had a report of an armed woman, had to take precautions. But I've done nothing wrong. Felicia asked me to take her to get something to eat, and I obliged." Still no response. Now she was getting pissed off. "This is bordering on harassment and false imprisonment. Please remove the cuffs, and I will explain everything."

He remained silent. But his partner tossed Lucy's bag onto the hood of the cruiser and began rummaging through it. He pulled out Carter's rainbow of folders.

"Those are confidential case files," she protested. She rose up onto her knees to see better, but the cop behind her shoved her back down, planting a boot on one shoulder.

Lucy inhaled mud. Gravel bit into her lip. Suddenly, both men were on her—the first restraining her while the second applied zip ties to her ankles, connecting them to her handcuffs, effectively hog-tying her. A position used for subjects who resisted arrest violently or who posed extreme danger to law enforcement officers.

She sighed. There was no reasoning with these men. They'd known the exact outcome of the encounter before they even stopped her car. Following Gold's orders, no doubt. She didn't fight back as they hauled her up and slid her face down onto the plastic rear bench in the back of a cruiser, wrapping the seat belt around her to secure her. Fury seethed through her. This was beyond insulting or a message of intimidation sent by Marcus Gold. These men, sworn officers, were abusing the power they were given under the color of the law. They'd sworn the same oath as Lucy had, and they were betraying it.

As they drove—Lucy was unable to see anything to help her identify their destination, but she assumed it was the Finely PD—she rehearsed speeches in her mind. Her first call would be to Valencia, a former civil rights attorney. This town wouldn't know what hit it once Lucy unleashed Valencia Frazier on them.

If Felicia was right and Marcus Gold owned Finely, then she'd make him pay for what he'd done today. The sense of righteous indignation burned through her, helping to quell some of her shame and embarrassment—not that she had anything to be ashamed of, but it was humiliating being treated like a common criminal, powerless.

But they kept driving. Much, much longer than

it would take to cross the tiny speck on the map that was Finely.

Lucy's rage gave way to fear. The way they'd taken her—as if they'd done it before. Could these be the same men who'd taken Alina that day in front of the courthouse? Was Hunt right that Marcus Gold was a rapist and a killer?

A man so rich and powerful that he'd grown bored, needed more excitement, more risk. But not too much—he'd need to be able to cover his tracks. So he'd developed a drug designed to cause amnesia, tested it on his first victims—Lucy's witnesses and Judith Miller—fine-tuned the dosage, whatever. And then...

She closed her eyes but couldn't block out the images of Alina's injuries. No empathy, Felicia had said while describing her youngest son. A charismatic psychopath, Hunt had diagnosed.

A man like that...no rules, no boundaries, no limits. He wouldn't stop. Wouldn't flinch at targeting anyone who got too close to the truth, not even a former federal agent. Wouldn't think twice about buying a police department to fetch his victims for him. Her breath came faster, gagging her with the stench of disinfectant and, underlying it, another more primal scent that had permeated the police car's seat: the smell of fear.

Where were they taking her? And who was waiting at the end of the road?

Chapter 21

Cassie sat in silence as Stefi drove them out of town. Stefi wasn't exactly silent, more like mumbling to herself as she tried to process what they'd just learned.

"I can't go to my boss with this," she finally said as they turned onto the interstate.

"Just because the guy is rich and famous doesn't mean—"

"We have no evidence."

"Stefi, he's linked to three of our victims. That can't be coincidence."

"Possibly linked—we need to verify everything Tandi just told us. And there's no physical evidence. Maybe it's not Gold. Maybe it's someone who planted that idea, impersonated him."

"Why?"

"I don't know. Could be someone who worked for him and has a grudge. Or who has access to his employee database and figures he can get away with targeting women linked to Gold because no one in their right mind would ever try to charge Gold, much less prosecute him. Or maybe—" She trailed off, weaving through traffic with a practiced hand.

"Maybe what?" Cassie finally asked.

"Okay, this is going to sound crazy, but we're starting from scratch, no assumptions." Stefi glanced at Cassie. "We know there's more than one person involved, because two men took Alina from the courthouse."

"Right. Doesn't mean they couldn't have been following Gold's orders. Man's rich enough to buy his own army."

"Exactly. And his company is going public soon—they've been talking about it for two years, building up anticipation. They say it's going to be the largest IPO in history. What if all this—" She hesitated, but Cassie saw where she was going.

"Someone wants to destroy Marcus Gold's company? Ruin his reputation, bring down the value before the IPO? You think someone paid Tandi to accuse Marcus? Used her rape? And now she's using us to get the word out, to implicate Marcus Gold?"

Stefi frowned. "Maybe. Or maybe they're behind the assaults? Chose victims with ties to Gold?"

"That's—"

"Crazy, I know. But that's also why it would work. I mean, anyone with enough money to tank Gold's IPO, sweep in and buy up stock when it's at a low, take control of the company... they're playing at a level way beyond anything I've ever seen before.

Men like that—"

"Wouldn't care about the women they destroyed along the way." Cassie's tone was bitter. She couldn't help but think of her first husband. He'd been rich, ruthless, and just as brutal as the men Stefi was describing.

"Again, just looking at every possibility. But something about these attacks has always felt off. I don't know, staged. I mean... What if Marcus Gold is also a victim?"

Cassie blew her breath out. "We've no proof for any of this."

"My point exactly. We have no proof at all—any defense attorney would rip apart Tandi's testimony, say the drugs made her imagine she saw Marcus. But I guess what all this conjecture comes down to is, this doesn't feel like a normal serial rapist. This actor, he's driven by something beyond power and rage and a need for control. There's something we aren't seeing."

"So we keep digging."

"Yes. But now more carefully than ever. For the sakes of the survivors as well as our own."

"And Alina's baby? Where does he fit into all this?"

Stefi's shrug didn't provide any comfort. Cassie couldn't help but notice how Alina's baby—out there somewhere, vulnerable, innocent, no matter the sins of his father—kept getting forgotten.

"Finding Alina's rapist is the key to finding the baby," Stefi finally said.

"You know, if your theory is right, then whoever

might be targeting Marcus Gold could have hired several men to do the attacks—gave them a script to follow, the drugs to use, knowing that with no physical evidence, we'd have to rely on circumstantial evidence like the lack of confirmed alibis. But if it's more than one man—"

"They'd have alibis for all the rapes except the one they committed. Talk about warped. I mean, who even thinks like that? And what kind of man would be willing to do that just for a paycheck?"

"The same kind of man willing to destroy seven women's lives for money." Cassie shook her head. "Is it strange that I actually now want it to be a single man? Someone so angry at women that I could understand his obsession? Because if all this is just about greed—"

"I don't want to live in a world where that's possible."

"Exactly."

"Let's start by seeing if Gold has ties to the other four victims. Then we can go from there."

As they drove, Cassie searched the internet for the video Tandi had mentioned, the one featuring their fifth victim, Anne Dawson. They were almost back to the city by the time she finally found it—an innocuous video featuring the accomplishments of various Marcus Gold employees. Anne apparently had brokered real estate deals that allowed Gold's company to expand globally. Cassie muted the boring award speech, focusing on Anne and the people around her. Then she sat up, tightening her grip on her phone.

"I found it," she told Stefi. "Why Alina was targeted."

"What?" Stefi was fighting traffic heading into the city and couldn't do more than glance in Cassie's direction.

"She was there, at the ceremony—one of the models who carried the trophies onto the stage to be handed to the winners. And the advertising agency Alina worked for produced the video."

"So now we have a connection to four out of seven." Stefi's expression turned grim. "This case just got bigger. Bigger than me, bigger than the Pittsburgh Police. Whatever we do next, we're poking a hornet's nest."

"Are you backing out?"

Stefi considered Cassie's question carefully. "No. No, I'm not."

Cassie's cell rang.

"It's Wash," he said. "From Beacon Falls." He sounded out of breath. "Have you heard anything from Lucy?"

"Not since she walked out on us this morning, but Drake texted that he had some info she was looking for on a traffic fatality. Guess he couldn't reach her. Why?" She put the phone on speaker so Stefi could listen as she drove.

"She called. But when the call connected, she wasn't there. All I could hear was what sounded like maybe the police arresting her? I'm not sure—I only heard a man telling her to keep her hands up, didn't hear anyone say they were police, so maybe they weren't."

"Do you have a location?" Stefi asked as she and Cassie exchanged worried glances.

"Just outside a little town named Finely. That's where she was anyway. Her cell's off, and they must have taken the battery out, too—I can't get any GPS."

"What about her vehicle? Do you have GPS on it?"

"It hasn't moved."

"Why was Lucy there?" Cassie asked. "Who'd she go see after she left us?"

"She went to see the US attorney, Graham Hunt. Those first two victims? The dead Jane Does? They were witnesses in a case Lucy was involved in when she was with the FBI. And then she went to see victim number three, Judith Miller—she lives in Finely." He paused for a breath. "Valencia is coordinating with the police. Finely has a small department. They said they have no record of Lucy or a traffic stop. They're taking her car to impound for safekeeping. The Staties don't have anything either." His tone grew taut with worry. "What if that's how the guy gets them? His victims? What if he pretends to be a cop? What if he took Lucy?"

"What can we do to help?" Cassie asked. "We're heading back into the city."

"Graham Hunt has pull with the feds. Valencia asked if you could head there, fill him in on our case so we can coordinate?"

"Will do," Stefi answered. "Have Detective

Drake meet us—if this traffic fatality is tied to our case, Hunt will want to know."

"Hey, Wash," Cassie started, uncertain if the tech analyst was the right person to share information with, especially information this sensitive. "Does Marcus Gold have any ties to our other victims?"

"Marcus Gold? Like, the Marcus Gold? The billionaire?"

"Just check for me, please? Discreetly."

"Yeah, sure. I'll get back to you if I find anything."

"Thanks."

Cassie turned to Stefi. "What if they weren't police? What if you're right? Why would they take Lucy?"

Stefi's hand left the steering wheel to brush against the gun holstered at her side. "Maybe Lucy got too close to the truth. Or maybe they want to know how much we know."

The images of their first two victims, the ones who were tortured, filled Cassie's vision. "We have to find her. Fast."

"As soon as they get the answers they want—" Stefi broke off.

But Cassie knew exactly what she was going to say. "They'll kill her."

Chapter 22

At first, Lucy tried to track the car's position, counting turns and length of time, but as the ride lengthened, she realized that there was no way the map in her head could match reality. Plus, it was pretty obvious that wherever the police officer was taking her, he wasn't taking a direct route.

He didn't make a sound the entire way—refused to answer her questions, even had his radio turned off, depriving her of another source of information. She realized that although she'd gotten a glimpse of his partner in the second car, she had no idea what her abductor looked like.

She spent the time trying every meditation technique Nick had taught her—not easy with her arms and legs cramping and her body sliding along the seat with every bump and turn. But it kept her fear at bay, giving her one small triumph over an impossible situation. Because fear was what this guy wanted, she knew. To intimidate, dominate, humiliate.

No way in hell was she giving him any of that. It

was a point of pride if nothing else.

Finally, he drove through several gates, then the car bumped over a change in the pavement and came to a stop, an automatic gate or door rattling down behind them. The driver turned the car off and got out. Even craning her head as high as she could, she couldn't see anything beyond blank concrete block walls.

"Got one," the driver told an unseen person.

"This the Finely package?" another man asked, sounding bored.

"Yep. Resisting arrest, kidnapping, suspected domestic terrorism, terroristic threats, and extortion of a civilian with access to classified information impacting national security." He listed the crimes as if they were a shopping list he'd memorized, and she wondered how many times, and to whom, these men had done this before. Because there was only one place an arrestee facing charges that severe would go: a federal detention center.

Her mind raced. Usually, if locals arrested someone the FBI was interested in, they used a detention cell in a federal building. But both the US Marshals and Homeland also had contracts with private facilities, as well as local county jails, where prisoners could be detained when needed.

A few minutes later, the car door opened, and a man leaned in behind her, snipping the zip cuffs free from her ankles, then hauling her backwards out of the car. Her legs felt leaden, despite sparking with pins and needles, unable to fully support her. The unseen man leaned her against the side of the cruiser and pressed her there with one hand braced between her shoulder blades while he removed her handcuffs. She heard the clink of metal chains as a second man locked her ankles into restraints, then circled her waist with a thick leather belt. After the first man released her, the second spun her around to face him, securing her wrists with a new set of cuffs attached to the belt. The Finely cop returned to the driver side of the car, still anonymous.

"My name is Lucy Guardino," she told the new man who wore a balaclava to hide his features and a drab green uniform with no insignia. "I'm a retired FBI agent and I've been unlawfully detained."

The guard made no reply. She glanced around. They were in a garage bay with a sally port leading inside the facility and a glass-walled intake area where two more masked men watched. Another stood at the doorway and held an M5 carbine, following her movements.

As her guard forced Lucy to shuffle forward as fast as her manacled legs would take her, she spotted a small plaque at the base of the observation window: A Marcus Gold Property. Laughter almost overcame her, but she stifled it. Despite everything, she couldn't help but appreciate the irony. Marcus Gold didn't merely own the land and building, he owned everyone inside... including Lucy. Such hubris, such narcissism. Damn, she was going to enjoy taking him down.

The intake process was similar to any prison facility: fingerprints, photos, strip search, change into institutional clothing—in this case, bright orange top and bottoms with flimsy slippers. Lucy tried to ignore the humiliation of being treated like cattle, but the fact that she saw no one else—and would not be able to identify her mostly silent captors—was more unnerving than she'd anticipated. There were others in the facility—she could hear distant sounds of babies crying, people shouting—but in this wing, there was only Lucy and the four guards.

The cell they locked her in was designed for one prisoner. There was a metal bench bolted to the concrete block wall, a thin mattress, a combo sink-toilet, an overhead light and monitoring camera, and that was it. Lucy fought not to wince as the steel door clanged shut, removing her final contact with the world outside. Nothing to do now but wait.

Except waiting was the one skill set Lucy had never mastered. Especially not now when her anger and humiliation and fear had coiled into a mass of lava in the pit of her belly, making her want to howl with rage. And she couldn't. Because that would mean they—whoever they were—won.

She sat on the naked mattress—no pillow, no sheets or blankets—folded her legs, rested her hands on her knees, and pretended to meditate. As if she accepted that there was no escape. As if her mind wasn't racing as she worried about the others on her team, about Nick and Megan, wondering who else Marcus Gold might decide to abduct and unlawfully imprison.

All she'd done was try to take an old woman out

to lunch. Who else would pay the price?

And she was powerless to warn them or stop anything from happening. That was the worst part.

After a while, the meal slot clanged open, and a tray slid into her cell. As if she'd ever risk eating any food that might be tainted by Marcus Gold's drugs. She ignored it. How foolish did they think she was?

They must have had her on suicide watch or the like, because despite the passage of time, the lights in her cell never went off. Or they simply wanted to disorient her—sleep deprivation was top of the list in preparing a subject for interrogation.

The cell was cold enough that she couldn't stop shivering. She was half tempted to roll the thin mattress around her, but again her pride stopped her. Instead, she did some pushups and jogged in place, keeping the blood flowing to her chilled limbs.

As she moved, her mind also kept busy. Not dwelling on her impossible situation but on the case. And she finally realized the one thing that had been bothering her ever since she'd learned the fate of her two missing witnesses, Fatima and Maria.

They'd been interrogated—tortured and interrogated, cartel style, according to TK and Jared Estanza. What had Hunt speculated? That their deaths were meant to appease the cartel working with the traffickers?

Except... Those men were willing to sell women over and over, treat them worse than animals, kill them when they were no longer profitable... So why give Fatima and Maria opioids? Enough to block the pain and cause an overdose?

The only answer could be that whoever had abducted and killed Fatima and Maria hadn't wanted them to suffer.

But then, why also give them the designer drug to cause amnesia? It was pretty clear from the high levels of opioids and the extreme trauma the women had suffered that they were meant to die. There had been no need to induce amnesia—they weren't going to live to say or remember anything.

She paused halfway up during a pushup, holding her body rigid as her mind raced. Unless... The designer drug had been given only so it'd show up in the autopsy. Which meant someone wanted all the cases to be linked eventually—from the very first two victims.

Someone had deliberately left a trail of breadcrumbs that would sooner or later lead right to Marcus Gold.

Chapter 23

CASSIE WAS RELIEVED TO SEE Drake's Mustang already parked in the circular driveway in front of the Hunts' mansion. With Drake on the case, the search for Lucy was in good hands.

A woman greeted them at the door, obviously Graham Hunt's wife. "Rebekah," she introduced herself. "Let me take you to the others."

"Any news?" Cassie asked before thinking better of it—someone would have called with good news. It was only bad news that you waited to deliver in person.

"I'm afraid not. But Graham's already gotten the FBI and State Police involved." They continued through a labyrinth of hallways that Cassie was certain she'd never be able to navigate back to the front door. "You know, I met her. Lucy. She was at the house this morning. We'd just gotten back from the pediatrician's."

"How old are your kids?" Stefi asked.

"Just the one. He's two weeks old."

"Oh, a newborn. I miss that—so sweet and cuddly," Stefi said, and Cassie realized she had no idea if the detective was married or had children of her own. Given her workload, how could she manage a partner and kids? But, from what she'd seen of Stefi, there seemed to be nothing the detective couldn't tackle, although Cassie had the sudden vision of onesies color-coded for each day of the week.

Rebekah led them to a door and knocked. It opened onto a large rec room repurposed as a command center. Cassie hesitated, watching as Stefi jumped into the fray, dumping her load of folders and bag onto a large banquet table before introducing herself. Then Drake saw Cassie and waved to her from across the room where he and another man were scrutinizing a map.

With the instincts of a good hostess, Rebekah seemed to sense Cassie's reluctance to intrude. After all, she had no professional law enforcement experience—she was here only as Alina's physician and friend.

"The young guy with the broad shoulders is Jared Estanza. He's an investigator from Homeland Security," Rebekah told Cassie. "He and my husband, the man in the blue shirt and tie, have spent more hours cooped up in this room—you wouldn't believe. Graham says they're close to a breakthrough. I think that's what Lucy was helping with when she was here this morning." She shrugged. "It's all classified, above a wife's pay grade. But you're probably used to that with your husband being a detective."

Actually, Drake shared a lot of his cases with Cassie, asking her opinion, appreciating her insights as a sounding board. But it seemed a sore point, Rebekah being excluded from such a large part of her husband's life, so Cassie merely nodded.

"I'm telling you, it has to be Marcus Gold," the Homeland investigator, Jared, said in a loud voice, as if he and Drake were arguing.

"Just saying," Drake replied, "I'm seeing a lot of interesting facts but no direct evidence to implicate Gold."

"Maybe I can help," Stefi said, drawing the attention of all the men. "Dr. Hart and I just came from interviewing one of the victims."

"How about if everyone takes a seat, and we'll go through things step by step?" Graham Hunt's baritone was warm and soothing.

Rebekah nodded to her husband. "Honey, should I get your guests some refreshments?" she said in a too-bland tone that Cassie translated as, We need to talk. Sure enough, Graham escorted Rebekah to the hall outside the room.

Cassie didn't mean to eavesdrop, but they didn't close the door the entire way. Rebekah said, "You're telling them it was Marcus Gold? Is that wise? You know what he's capable of."

"I've got it covered, don't worry."

"Don't worry?" Her tone cut sharper than carbon steel. "Don't you dare tell me not to worry, not after—"

"I told you, I've got everything under control.

You know I'll do whatever it takes to keep you and the baby safe." Their voices faded as they moved away from the door. As Drake and the others gathered around the table, heads together as they talked, Cassie strolled around the room's perimeter. In the far corner, she found a stack of campaign posters along with placards and trifolds. Apparently, Graham Hunt was planning to run for Senate. She picked up a brochure, glancing at the happy photos of Graham and Rebekah, a serious headshot of the candidate, and a photo of him in action in court, appearing like a champion of justice. Then she saw the tiny copyright notice and logo at the bottom. The brochures had been created several months ago by the same ad agency Alina had worked for.

Alina had been fired around the same time because her pregnancy was showing. The thought of Alina's baby made her think of Rebekah and Graham's son. Funny, Rebekah didn't look pregnant in any of these photos. Maybe they were old. Or maybe Cassie was simply so desperate to find Alina's baby that any infant male was catching her attention, making her suspicious.

Before she could think any more of it, Graham returned. "Valencia just called from Finely," he announced. "There's no sign of Lucy anywhere, nothing helpful in her car. But we now know who Lucy went to see after she left Judith Miller's." He paused, waiting for everyone's gazes to settle on him. "Lucy was last seen interviewing Felicia Gold. Marcus Gold's mother."

That got a reaction from the investigators. Jared Estanza did a fist pump into the air. Stefi's head bobbed as she opened her laptop and began typing furiously. And Drake turned to Hart, a concerned look on his face.

Graham Hunt stood still, his gaze sweeping the walls of the room with their crime scene photos and timelines. "It's no cause for celebration," he said in a grim tone. "We don't know where Lucy's been taken. Gold is a man who holds himself above the law and has the resources to remove anyone he sees as a threat."

"But we got him," Jared protested.

"Circumstantial," Drake said. "Nothing that would ever hold up in court."

"I'm afraid Detective Drake is right," Graham said, finally joining the others at the table. Leaving Cassie the only person standing beyond their intimate circle.

"Dr. Hart and I have discovered connections between Marcus Gold and four of our victims," Stefi said. "And we now know he's connected to the first three as well."

Cassie stood, anger building inside her at how blind these extremely smart and capable detectives were. So driven to build their case, they were missing the obvious.

"If Marcus Gold took Lucy," she said, straining to keep her voice level. They wouldn't take her seriously if she sounded overly emotional. But dammit, she was. "Then he knows we're on to him.

He's capable of abducting a former FBI agent, despite the manhunt he has to know that would trigger."

The words caught in her throat. She took a breath as the others stared at her, the outsider, the non-law-enforcement professional. Even Drake, who could usually guess her thoughts and feelings just by looking at her, didn't see what was so blindingly obvious to Cassie.

"A man like that," she continued. "Why would he keep the one concrete piece of evidence against him now that he knows you're on to him? Why would he keep Alina's baby alive?"

Chapter 24

Lucy passed the night feeling like a caged animal. It was too cold in the cell to sleep, not to mention the blazing lights and knowledge that she was under constant surveillance. A wasted effort on behalf of her captors. Even if it had been cozy, warm, and dark, she never would have allowed her guard to drop enough to sleep anyway.

With morning came another tray of food that she ignored, despite the enticing aroma of institutional artificial eggs. A short time later, the door to her cell opened, and a masked guard gestured for her to accompany him. A tickle of hope rose when he didn't restrain her, and she kept her gaze sharp, searching for any possible escape.

It was a short reprieve as he ushered her through a maze of corridors connected by secured gates that they had to wait to be buzzed through. Suddenly, they emerged into a corridor lined with windows on one side, the early morning sun making her blink. Then he knocked politely on the wooden door of a room before opening it and nodding to Lucy to enter.

The paneled conference room could have been at home in any of a thousand office buildings, with its generic abstract paintings and featureless oval table and chairs. At the head of the table sat a man reading something on his phone. He had the whippet-thin frame of a long-distance runner and the gaunt, hollowed cheeks and dark circles of a chronic insomniac. Marcus Gold, the great man himself.

He gestured to the chair at the far end of the table, the one reserved for the lowest ranking. Instead, she strolled across the room and took the seat immediately to his right—putting her in position to take control of his strong hand, if need be. He ignored her power play, never glancing up from his phone.

"I have to confess, after reading your file, I was looking forward to meeting you, Lucy. But now—" He sighed. "I'm a bit underwhelmed. Here I was, expecting a hero, and instead I get—" Finally, he looked up at her, raising an eyebrow, indicating Lucy's bedraggled appearance. "I get a disheveled housewife playing at detective."

Let him try going with no sleep or food for a day and see how he looked, Lucy wanted to retort. Instead, she matched her expression to his own. "I know the feeling. After hearing about the great Marcus Gold, imagine my own...disappointment."

"I didn't fly halfway around the world, canceling meetings with heads of state and the Pope himself, just to be insulted."

"I didn't expect a renowned humanitarian such as yourself to kidnap and imprison someone trying to stop a sexual predator. For merely doing his mother a kindness."

"Oh, is that what you were doing? Or were you trying to get a frail old woman to dish up the dirt on her famous son, the one she takes every opportunity to call a disappointment? Despite the fact that she'd probably be dead by now if it weren't for me."

Felicia was obviously Gold's weak spot, so Lucy kept pushing at it. "Have you seen her house? If she's so frail, why haven't you moved her to someplace decent?"

"If she had it her way, my mother would let that damn house fall down around her before she accepted my help. And if I ever forced her to move, she'd be shouting 'abuse' from the rooftops. So I do my best to make sure she's safe and taken care of—and that her privacy is protected."

"You mean your privacy. Felicia never asked me to leave. In fact, she asked me to take her out to lunch. No harm in that—except maybe it meant we could have a conversation beyond the range of your monitoring." It was a guess, but given how fast the cops had arrived, Lucy bet it was a good one.

"My mother is a diabetic with strict dietary needs. I was merely protecting her from another medical crisis."

"Protecting her meant kidnapping and falsely imprisoning me?" She leaned forward. "Tell me, Mr. Gold, what exactly are you afraid of? What kind of threat does this 'disheveled housewife' pose to a great man like yourself?"

He stared at her, lips tight, but he didn't take the bait. She could see that his restraint was requiring effort, so she pushed further. "Were you afraid that I'd learn you were behind the attacks on seven women? Sexual assaults so heinous that, if the public knew you were behind them, you could lose everything."

Now he smiled, showing his teeth—unnaturally white and flawless. "I have an alibi."

"You know the exact dates of all the attacks?"

"No. Makes no difference. I have an alibi for any day you ask about."

Of course he did. Man that rich, he could buy multiple alibis easily.

"Don't misunderstand me," he continued, seeing the skepticism she couldn't hide. "Nothing nefarious. Just saying—I travel all over the world. Chances of me being anywhere near these parts at the time of the attacks, well, they're slim to none. I don't get back home much."

"Not even to visit your mother?" Lucy knew she was overstepping an unsaid boundary, but she wanted to see his reaction.

"I'd happily visit my mother. Anytime she asks." He let that hang for a moment. "I'd love to come back home." His tone turned wistful.

Home? More like prison. But Felicia's situation was beyond Lucy's purview. "You have a degree in pharmacy, right?"

"Along with a doctorate in biochemistry. Why?"

"My case. It involves a designer drug, some kind of hybrid between GHB and rohypnol."

"Ah, yes, you mentioned investigating a case." He made her work sound sordid and sullied, as if he was too good to involve himself in such things. "Tell me, how did this drug perform?"

"It devastated Judith Miller. I'm sure your mother mentioned that she's lost her entire life, back to when she was a child. Can't make new memories. It's as if her life has been erased, leaving her an empty shell."

"Interesting." A bemused smirk flitted over his face. An expression of childish satisfaction that the life of the woman who'd rejected him had been destroyed. Below the table, Lucy clenched her fist—it was the only way to keep from slapping him.

A silence hung between them, Lucy waiting, hoping he'd be moved to fill it. When he didn't, she asked, "Is that why you created the drug? For your own private amusement, getting revenge on women who threaten you?"

"You obviously have no idea how many projects my various companies are undertaking at any one time. Not to mention all the research we support." He leaned back in his seat, legs spread wide. "I assure you, if this drug came from one of my companies or subsidiaries, I had no knowledge of it or its unfortunate side effects until today."

"Of course. I just thought, given that you were so close to at least one of the victims, you might have taken a personal interest."

"Poor Judi. I haven't seen or thought of her in years. But now that you've brought it to my attention, I'll certainly take a look. Maybe we could even come up with a treatment." He spoke with an academic detachment.

"Do you remember Graham Hunt? You went to college with him."

"Graham?" His frown was melodramatic—as if Lucy needed yet another indication that he was lying. "Vaguely. You need to understand, Lucy, I was so much younger and smarter than the other guys at school. It was obvious to anyone that I was going places, while the rest of them relied on their inbred traditions and trust funds." Then he sat up straighter. "Graham Hunt...I might remember him after all. Only because of the girl we both went after. Rebekah Kaufmann—yes, one of those Kaufmanns. She chose me, of course. Despite the fact that I was a penniless scholarship student. Rebekah saw my potential. Graham was so jealous, caused a bit of a stir, almost got me kicked out of school." He leaned back once more, a smile flitting across his face at the memory. "But it all got sorted out in the end. And I moved on to greener pastures."

Meaning the extortion Hunt had alluded to? Or was Hunt delusional, driven by jealousy? There was something between the two men, something deep and primal. Rebekah?

"You know he married Rebekah, right? They just had a baby." She watched, hoping for a slip of emotion, but his expression remained placid.

"Really? I'm surprised to hear that—the baby, not the marriage."

"Why are you surprised?"

His expression turned haughty. "Because I happen to know that Rebekah kicked Graham out of their bedroom after he almost got her killed when he ran their car off the road. They lost their unborn child as a result, and Rebekah was partially paralyzed." He seemed to know a lot about a couple he professed to barely remembering, but Lucy wanted to keep him talking so didn't challenge him on his inconsistencies. "Graham came to me, asking, begging for help. It was one of my stem-cell therapies that enabled Rebekah to walk again."

"So I guess he owes you?" Certain to drive a man like Hunt crazy.

"To any other man, that would present a debt of honor." His gaze narrowed. "Not necessarily to Graham Hunt, though. Probably best that he ended his campaign for the Senate. I'd hate to think of a man like that in power."

"What do you mean?"

"Graham was drinking the night of the accident, but he had it covered up. Rebekah was lying in a coma, paralyzed, near to death, their unborn child is dead, and all dear Graham could think about was how to avoid responsibility. Shameless."

The accident was Hunt's fault? Hadn't he said Gold was trying to kill him? Lucy made a mental note to ask Drake to check out the police reports.

"You know, he's running for Senate again." She waited for his reaction. "Planning to be on the ballot for the next election."

For the first time, he seemed startled. Leaned forward in his chair, shoulders hunched. "Is he, now? We'll see about that." His gaze went distant for a moment, then he nodded to himself. "Well, now, I'm afraid that's all the time I have to spare for this little...misunderstanding."

He stood, tossing a business card on the table. "I understand your daughter, Megan, is doing a project on gene editing. Tell her to give my assistant a call. We'll get her a behind-the-scenes tour of our Pittsburgh lab. It will blow her teacher away. Guaranteed A-plus."

Lucy fought to keep the emotion from her face. How the hell did he know what Megan was working on in school? And in less than twenty-four hours since Lucy appeared on Gold's radar?

A shudder raced over her—Gold's intended result of his offhand exit line. He wanted her to know he could reach her and everyone she loved at a moment's notice.

It was a threat she would not ignore. Or forgive.

CHAPTER 25

AFTER ALLOWING HER TO CHANGE back into her own clothing, Gold's men had driven Lucy to the Finely PD, where her car and other belongings waited. There was no paperwork, no acknowledgment that anything had happened. No one at the police department even confessed to knowing who she was or why her car was in their parking lot.

Lucy eyed her Subaru with suspicion. Even though she'd only been held overnight, it was more than enough time to wire the car with surveillance. Her phone would be compromised as well, along with anyone in her contacts. They would have found her burner phone, so it was now useless. She blew her breath out, unlocked the driver's door, and got in. She'd just have to find a way to use Gold's bugs against him.

She sat in the car and checked her texts and voicemails. As expected, her family and friends from Beacon Falls had been trying to reach her. She even had one from Graham Hunt. But then came the final voicemail, timed at four eleven in the morning, from Judi Miller's mother.

"What have you done?" Bernice was practically shrieking. "All Felicia ever wanted was to be left alone, to have some peace and quiet away from her son, but now she's gone! And someone has burned her house down. That house was everything to her, but now everything, it's all gone. Thanks to you. Her son can do anything he wants with her now, so I hope whatever she told you was worth it. Don't ever come near me or my family again, you hear me? Never!"

Lucy stared at her phone as if it was a snake ready to strike. If Marcus Gold burned down his own mother's home just to punish her for daring to speak with Lucy, then what would Gold do if Lucy persisted in her search for the truth?

Who among her friends and family would he target? Could she risk it?

Lucy headed toward home, taking a circuitous route to make sure she wasn't followed—although she was certain there was more than one GPS tracker on her car and belongings in addition to her phone. But it was important to act as if she didn't know that.

She pulled into a truck stop just outside of the city. After downing eggs, sausage, and two single-serve cartons of milk, she bought a few provisions and headed to the women's restroom.

Lucy waited until the restroom was empty to use one of the four burner phones she'd bought to dial another, then used that phone to conference in a third number—one of the few numbers she had memorized:

Timmy Oshiro's burner number. Like her, the Deputy US marshal had dealt with threats to his family in the past and always remained vigilant, knowing how easy it was for the bad guys to target a known cell number.

"Who is this?" he answered gruffly.

"It's me. I need your help—your old kind of help." Before joining the FAST team, Oshiro had had a brief stint in WITSEC. Until he'd grown bored of coddling criminals and wanted to go back to catching them. "I kicked a hornet's nest, Timmy. You remember that Armenian mob guy you told me about?"

"Yeah. Cross him, he wouldn't just kill you and your family, he'd go after your neighbors, your family's family as far back as it went, your pizza-delivery guy, and when there was no one left standing, he'd shoot your dog."

"That's what I'm up against."

"Who?"

She hauled in a breath, told him everything, including about her imprisonment, which she was certain would be mysteriously erased from any logs, as if it never happened.

"Wherever they held you, it wasn't one of ours," he assured her. "Must've been ICE or Homeland working with a private contractor."

"Right now, I don't really care about the assholes who ruined my beauty sleep," she snapped. "If Gold's behind all this, who knows where it goes? Our victims might be the tip of the iceberg."

"And Hunt? Where's he fit in?"

"Not sure. He could be working with Gold or against Gold. All I know is that Homeland and ICE are compromised, and Hunt's investigator, Jared Estanza, is HSI. He had access to every witness, including Fatima and Maria—" She made a note to find a way to talk to Drake, see what he'd learned about the accountant's death.

"First things first, let's get your family safe. I'll start making travel arrangements. Give me a few hours. We got that much time?"

"Yeah, I'll give them a wild-goose chase, keep them focused on me. Maybe I'll head over to Hunt's, get a read on his and Estanza's reactions."

"Don't take any unnecessary chances. You can't trust anyone."

"I'm pissed off, not stupid."

"Just saying, I've been there."

"I know. You might want to think about June and the baby—they'll know you and I are tight."

"Way ahead of you."

"They've had my car and phone since yesterday."

"So assume everyone is compromised." He thought for a moment. "We'll need at least two clean vehicles, but they'll be suspicious when Nick suddenly leaves his. Maybe he takes it in for repairs? That'd be a good pickup spot, behind closed doors. I know just the place—"

"Good," she cut him off before he could give her specifics. The less she knew, the safer Nick and Megan would be. "I'll call Nick, give him a heads-up, have him reach out to you from a secure phone. And, Timmy?" She swallowed hard, fighting to stay in control. She knew this was the right thing to do, but still couldn't help feel, deep down in her bones, that it was a mistake to trust her family to someone else. "It'll just be Nick and Megan going with. I can't, not with a target on my back."

There was a long pause before he answered. "I get it, but they won't."

"Whoever you send, have them tell them, 'Cantaloupes can't elope.' They'll know it's safe." Megan had chosen the family's code phrase years ago. She'd been in elementary school, obsessed with silly puns and riddles. At the time, it'd seemed overly paranoid, having a code that told Lucy's family to either follow her lead in a situation or blindly obey a stranger who knew the phrase.

Now those silly words might save the lives of her family.

Chapter 26

Cassie woke to the sound of a baby crying. At first, she thought she was still dreaming—her restless sleep had been filled with dreams of lost babies. Hers, Alina's, babies she'd delivered, babies she'd treated, somehow they all blurred together under the haze of sleep. They all needed her, and she was afraid that she'd failed them.

She rolled over, expecting to see Drake, but his side of the bed was cold and empty. She blinked, now fully awake. Sunshine slanted through the drapes of the Hunts' guest room. The baby cried again, and she remembered that the nursery was next door.

Hungry, she translated the cry as she climbed out of bed. She quickly used the bathroom, climbed back into the clothes she'd worn yesterday, and stumbled into the hallway just as Rebekah was coming down the hall carrying a bottle. Despite the early hour, and no doubt a sleepless night, given all her unexpected guests and a baby to care for, she still appeared fresh and ready for the day.

"I hope Jakob didn't wake you," she said when she saw Cassie. "I knew I should have put you in a room farther away from the nursery."

Cassie followed her into the baby's room. It was painted sky blue and had a nautical theme. A door led to a bathroom, and through the bath was another bedroom. Rebekah scooped the baby up, and he instantly quieted. She smushed a few kisses against his fat cheeks, then sat in the rocker and gave him the bottle. He gulped greedily at first, then slurped slower, eyes drifting shut in contentment.

"He's so beautiful," Cassie said, sitting on the love seat beside the rocker.

"I know. Every day, I pinch myself, can't believe he's mine."

"How do you do it? I mean, you look like you haven't missed a night's sleep."

"Honestly? Up until a few nights ago, I didn't. One of the joys of not having to breastfeed. A night nanny. Highly recommended."

Cassie gave a chuckle. Rebekah was so nice that she kept forgetting how rich the Hunts were.

"Do you and Detective Drake have children?"

It was the question that Cassie hadn't learned how to navigate yet. In her heart, the answer was a resounding yes. But to anyone else... "I was pregnant, earlier in the year. I lost it..." It was the first time she'd told anyone. Most of her friends didn't even know, and the ones who did, Drake had broken the news to them. "The baby...the baby died. Miscarriage."

None of the words felt right. But somehow it was easier telling a stranger, someone she'd probably never see again, someone...neutral.

Rebekah hugged Jakob closer, her gaze focused on her baby, anywhere but on Cassie. "I lost my first. Sarah. I was seven months. We were in a car crash that broke my pelvis, my back. There was bleeding they couldn't stop. They rushed me to surgery, but it was too late for Sarah."

"I'm so sorry you went through that. It must have been a nightmare."

"Took me a year to learn to walk again. Marcus, he paid for it all, cutting-edge treatments."

"You had a spinal cord injury?"

She nodded. "I know you all think Marcus is a bad man, but he's also a good man. I can't believe all the things Graham says he did, not after he helped us, helped me, regain my life."

Cassie couldn't help but think of the way Marcus Gold seemed one step ahead of them. How had he even gotten to Lucy so quickly yesterday? Unless someone who thought of him as a friend was feeding him information.

"And now you have everything," she said, uncertain how to steer the conversation without actually accusing Rebekah of anything.

"Thanks to Marcus and the miracles of modern medicine."

"You know what Graham's investigating? The women?"

Rebekah rocked faster as the baby slept against

her breast, the bottle empty. "I know." Her lips pressed together. "I think most men, they're easy to see who they are. Like my Graham. When he was a kid, he did anything his parents and grandparents told him to do, even if it wasn't the life he dreamed of—because his family came first. Now, he's the same way. Would do anything for family."

"But Marcus?"

She gave a little laugh. "Did you know Marcus and Graham went to school together? They were so damned competitive—over grades, over sports, over girls. They'd turn anything into a competition. When Graham and I got engaged, Marcus told me I was the only prize he'd ever lost."

"Seriously? As if you didn't have any say in the matter?" Definitely fit the way a serial rapist might view women.

"That's Marcus. He vowed never to lose to Graham again. Never to lose to anyone again. And he hasn't." She smiled at Cassie. "Like I said, men are easy to understand. Guess that's one of our secret weapons as women. Because once you understand them, you have the upper hand. Marcus and Graham, they treated me like I was Helen of Troy. In fact, Graham called me that in a love poem he once wrote way back when. Like I was a prize that they could choose and win. But they never realized I was the one doing the choosing."

"Can I ask? Why Graham and not Marcus?"

Rebekah's smile widened into a grin. "Marcus gets bored so easily, it could never last. So I went with loyal, steady Graham. But to Marcus, I'll always be the one who got away, so he'll never not be there for me when I need him."

"Like after the car accident."

"Exactly. Best of all worlds."

There was a knock on the door, and Drake appeared. "We just heard from Valencia. Lucy called. She's all right."

"Where was she? What happened?" Cassie asked.

"Apparently, she was in jail all night. A federal detention center." He glanced at the baby, softened his tone. "One owned and run by Marcus Gold."

"If Marcus can take someone off the street for no reason—" She swallowed hard, the implications roiling through her. Her gut reaction wasn't to run, but to edge closer to the baby. As if through sheer proximity, she could somehow protect him. "Then that means we're all targets."

CHAPTER 27

AFTER SHE'D LET VALENCIA know that she was safe and heading to Hunt's, Lucy was dreading her next call: explaining things to Nick. Over the years, he'd put up with a lot from her career and the way it occasionally placed a target on their family, but she'd never vanished for a full night before—or asked him to take Megan and go on the run until things calmed down.

Maybe she was overreacting. If so, fine. Better that Nick and Megan return home safe and sound and royally pissed off at her than the alternative.

Nick had his patient calls forwarded to his professional cell, a number that wasn't on Lucy's phone, so presumably was safe.

"Dr. Callahan," he answered on the second ring.

Lucy's words were caught, trapped by a sudden rush of emotion at the sound of his voice. She blinked back tears and tried again. "It's me."

His quick intake of breath echoed through the phone. "Are you all right?"

"I'm fine. A bit shaken is all. And angry as hell.

Take the dog out to the backyard so we can talk without anyone listening. The house might be bugged." Then she sketched out the relevant details, keeping them to simple bullet-point items, laying out her argument as unemotionally as possible.

"Where are we going?" he asked when she finished. No debate, no recriminations, simply prioritizing his family's safety. Lucy closed her eyes, sending a grateful prayer as she did most days, thankful that this man was hers.

Nick was no pushover, and there'd be hell to pay—a good three-day argument, she'd wager—but he wasn't about to waste precious time now, which she appreciated. Their marriage was a constant seesaw between his belief in humanity and her paranoia, but for now they were in agreement.

"Not we," she told him. "You and Megan. Grab your go-bags. Oshiro is going to call you with details on where to meet."

"So I get to spend a weekend with Oshiro and Megan practicing hand-to-hand combat and shooting at tin cans and whatnot—"

"June and the baby are coming as well," she put in. Nick actually enjoyed babysitting more than he'd ever admit—maybe because he and Megan had been the ones who delivered June's baby when she'd gone into labor unexpectedly.

"Okay. But what will you be doing?" Any other man would have allowed more than a hint of resentment to creep into his voice, but not Nick.

"Me?" She grinned, the burden of her family's

safety lifted. "I'm going to nail this bastard."

"You know, no one would think less of you if you came with us instead. Let the cops and feds do their jobs." He was using his neutral counseling tone—not telling her what to do, simply reminding her that there was always a choice.

"I would think less of me," she answered, just as she knew he knew she would. "But don't worry," she reassured him, knowing what he was really concerned about—that she'd let her fury cloud her judgment. "It's not because Gold's made this personal. Nick, if you'd seen that girl, Judi, what he did to her—and the others. Someone has to stop him. Now, before there's another victim."

"Okay, then." A sigh escaped him, betraying his emotions. "Guess we'll see you when we see you. Do me a favor. Be careful. I mean really, really careful. This guy, from what you've told me, he won't think twice—"

"I know. It's why I need you and Megan safe with Oshiro."

"I love you."

"Love you. And I promise I'll be careful." She hung up, already regretting her choice. But there really was no choice. This was who she was, and she didn't know any other way.

As she drove through the city, Lucy debated ditching her car, but after gaining access to her files, Gold already knew the intimate details of their investigation. Probably more, given his vast resources. He'd know Hunt was involved, so who cared if he tracked her there?

When she arrived, Cassandra Hart met her at the door and led her through the winding hallways to Hunt's rec room. As they walked, Hart told Lucy about their progress.

"So now we have connections between Marcus Gold and all the victims, including Alina," she finished. "But Graham says we need more evidence, that what we have isn't enough."

They walked into the room. Jared Estanza had his face buried in Carter's rainbow folders, Drake leaned against one wall talking on the phone, Carter typed furiously at her computer, and Hunt paced, a scowl clouding his face. The atmosphere was one of dejection combined with stubborn refusal to give up—emotions that often hit when a case entered the doldrums, which almost every case did eventually.

It was how you pushed past, opening new avenues of investigation, that determined the outcome, Lucy had learned over the years.

"No idea why you guys are looking so hangdog, I'm the one who spent the night under suicide watch courtesy of Homeland and Marcus Gold." She kept her tone bright and energetic. Sometimes you just had to fake it till you made it.

Estanza took the bait, as she'd hoped he would. "Homeland would've had nothing to do with that," he protested.

"I know. It was the Finely police. Well, two of them, at any rate. Apparently, Marcus Gold not only owns the town, but his company owns several private detention facilities. Contracted by Homeland and run by his people."

As Lucy told her story, Rebekah brought in lunch. Chili, fresh cornbread, salad and toppings. Despite her truck stop breakfast, Lucy was starving, but tried to focus on giving the others every detail that might help their investigation.

"Why take you and then just let you go?" Stefi asked when Lucy had finished.

"Main reason? I pissed him off." She remembered Bernice's message that Felicia's house had been burned down. "This guy doesn't know the meaning of anger management."

"Yeah, sounds like Marcus," Hunt put in. "He'd rather pick a fight he has no chance in hell of winning than ever admit defeat. And God help you if you did beat him—he loves his revenge served hot, cold, lukewarm—no matter to him."

"Gold made it very clear that this is personal, so I've arranged for my family to be taken to a safe house. Just saying, in case any of you need to make similar arrangements, this might be a good time. Because the other reason Gold had me taken was to allow him access to my computer and all our files. I'm sure he has my phone bugged, as well as my car, probably my laptop, too."

Hunt slammed a palm against the table, shaking it so hard that Estanza had to scramble to keep Carter's folders from cascading to the floor. "Then he knows everything we know. Dammit, he's always a step ahead."

"So let's use the opportunity, take a step back, and look at the big picture," Lucy continued. "How will Gold respond to the threat we pose? Personal attacks on our witnesses and families won't really solve his problem in the long term, will they?"

It was Drake who answered her. "He'll need a permanent solution that would silence his accusers. Forever."

"I asked Valencia to set up security for all our witnesses. But given their memory issues and the lack of forensic evidence, they're really not a huge threat to him. Is there a way to draw him out, force him to be reckless?" Her gaze fell on Hunt. "He seemed personally offended by your decision to run for Senate again." She didn't mention Gold's other accusations, about Hunt being drunk and causing the car crash that had almost killed Rebekah.

"He's got a charity fundraiser tonight. He always makes a point of inviting me and Rebekah, but we never go."

"Maybe tonight's the night," Carter said. "Seems like Gold puts a lot of stock in how he appears to the public. And with his company's IPO coming soon, he needs that positive public perception now more than ever." She turned to Lucy. "But I think we need to consider every angle here. What if Gold isn't the actor but the target? What if he's being set up? That might be why he's so pissed off, man like him. He'd see being a victim equivalent to being a loser, a failure."

As Carter explained her theory, Lucy wasn't

surprised to learn of Gold's involvement with the development of the amnesia drug or that he'd stolen it from a researcher. But she also wasn't sure she bought Carter's idea that this almost-three-year-long crime spree had been solely financially motivated. No. This felt personal, very personal.

"It would have to be someone who knows Gold intimately, in order to know about his connections with all the victims," Hart said.

"Someone like Tandi?" Carter asked. "She had plenty of motivation to try to destroy Gold's IPO along with his reputation."

"How did she—or anyone—know about our first two victims, the two involved with the trafficking ring Gold was leading?" Drake asked.

"Presumably leading," Carter said. She turned to Hunt. "Any chance your intel was wrong when it pointed to Gold's involvement with the cartel?"

"No," Hunt snapped.

Estanza jumped to Hunt's defense. "Our intel was solid until our witnesses ended up dead. And don't forget, Gold was also behind the massacre of my team."

Lucy thought about that. Whoever was responsible for their seven victims had access to Gold's designer drug, as well as the ability to either bribe or enlist ICE agents to help facilitate access to three of the victims. And was willing to do anything, even rape and kill innocent women, to destroy Gold.

There was one man she knew who might meet two out of the three criteria. Jared Estanza. Make that three out of three—anyone clever enough to pull this off could easily find a way to steal the designer drug.

"Does it even matter if Gold is being set up, or if he's our actor?" Hunt asked. "Although I don't see how anyone could believe him innocent of the sexual assaults and murders when we know he's involved in the trafficking. Plus, he had access to the designer drug, knew how to use it."

"Don't forget he also owns detention centers," Estanza put in. "Giving him access to ICE—or at least the means to impersonate their agents."

"Either way," Lucy said, "it's time to go on the offensive. So we use Gold—either as target or bait. But how?" She turned to Drake. "Was there anything from the CPA's death that we could use?"

He shook himself, and she realized that everyone was as exhausted and sleep deprived as she was. "Not sure. Maybe. The traffic accident seems to be exactly that, an accident. Jo Anderson couldn't find anything suspicious about the driver's actions. But when I told the ME that we were suspicious, he got curious. During the autopsy he found signs of asphyxiation and no signs of heart disease. I just got off the phone with him—he pulled in a favor, had a special tox screen run that found a lethal dose of aconitum in the victim's system. We got lucky. Any longer, and it would have been gone, never shown up."

"How long would that take to kill someone?" Lucy asked, excited that they finally had a new lead.

"ME said a few minutes, ten at most."

Carter bounced in her chair, pulling her laptop

closer. "We can retrace his steps, see if there's any video or witnesses—"

"I say we find what we can," Hunt said. "But even if we need to bluff, we confront Gold tonight at his little charity gala. We need to end this. Now. Today."

"We need to be careful," Lucy warned, concerned by the vehemence in Hunt's tone. He was too personally involved, letting his emotions rule his logic. "Travel in pairs, use burner phones, treat this as a red-level threat."

"Drake and I can work the street," Carter said. "Follow the accountant's steps."

Drake moved to stand beside his wife. "Hart, you'll be safest here."

"Definitely," Hunt said. "Please, Dr. Hart, make yourself at home. We can meet back here before the gala, decide upon a plan of attack." He leaned over the table, palms braced against it, looked them each in the eye. "This has gone too far for too long. No man is above the law. Not even Marcus Gold. Find me something. Anything we can nail him on."

Hart and Drake drifted out along with Carter. Hunt followed after them. Leaving Estanza and Lucy. Perfect. She'd wanted to get the HSI investigator alone—he had a lot of explaining to do.

Starting with why he'd lied to her about ICE deporting Fatima and Maria.

CHAPTER 28

LUCY DECIDED TO EASE into the subject of Fatima and Maria, start with a topic closer to Estanza's heart. She joined him at the far wall where a corkboard was dedicated to his team's ambush. "Tell me what happened."

He shrugged one shoulder, gaze cemented on the satellite image of the bodies of his team, obviously reluctant to talk about the deaths of his friends. "Like I said yesterday, it was an ambush. Only thankful thing was that the Zapatas didn't take anyone alive. Have you seen the videos of what those bastards do to prisoners?"

She had. What they did wasn't unlike how Fatima and Maria had been tortured. "How did you know Marcus Gold was behind it? I don't see anything here tying him to it. Did you track the false intel back to him?"

His jaw clenched at the mention of Gold's name. "No. If I had, he'd already be behind bars. But I know it was him who set us up. A drone filmed the whole thing—not ours. The video was uploaded to a secure IP address that was traced back to Marcus Gold."

Lucy frowned. It wasn't unusual for cartels to video their crimes—they used edited versions to instill fear, intimidate, and even to serve as accompaniments to their narco-ballads. But why would Marcus Gold want footage of a Border Patrol squad being massacred? And why target a squad that was nowhere near Gold's East Coast trafficking ring. How would that serve his interests?

"Who told you about the drone and the video footage?"

"Hunt. Found it while researching connections between Gold and the Zapatas for the trafficking RICO case. That's when he asked me to come on board as his investigator—he was concerned about possible ICE corruption. Working for the inspector general, I have more independence than most investigators."

"So he basically handed you Gold on a silver platter."

"No. Wasn't that easy. I've been working with Hunt for almost a year now, and we still haven't found who supplied the bad intel that set us up."

"Only a year? Then you weren't involved in the sex trafficking RICO case."

"Hunt wanted to focus on the trafficking ring for the grand jury, thought it'd be the easiest case to get an indictment on, but he was hoping to expand the scope of charges against Gold. Including possible terrorism charges if I could find evidence that Gold was funding or using the cartel as his personal assassins." He turned away from the photos to focus on her, his eyes going flat. "You don't really care about my squad."

"Why did you believe that my two witnesses were deported?" she challenged him. "You told me that, not Hunt."

"Obviously, I was wrong, given that we now know they're dead."

"We also now know that they were killed almost three years ago, before you came on the case."

"Right." Then he glanced at her, comprehension dawning. "Wait. You think ICE was involved with their deaths?"

She thought hard, wondering how far she could trust Estanza. The dates didn't add up. When Fatima and Maria were abducted and murdered, Estanza was in Texas with the Border Patrol—his squad was killed a few weeks after. "ICE knew where Fatima and Maria were living while they waited for their U visas. Who better to grab them and alter the database to say they were deported?"

"Hunt told me they were deported. I can ask him who gave him the information." He thought for a moment. "Those two men in ICE jackets, the ones who took Alina at the courthouse. Maybe Gold has his own men inside ICE, just like he owns the cops who grabbed you yesterday."

"Can you check without anyone getting suspicious? See what's in the database, who entered the data, who was out on operations on those dates?"

He thought for a moment, then nodded. "Yeah.

But I'll need to go to the DHS offices to access their secure system. Saturday afternoon, there won't be many in the office, and I have clearance to access everything we need. If anyone looks, though, they'll know I'm the one checking up on them."

Meaning she was basically asking Estanza to put a target on his own back. "Can you think of any other way to verify the data?"

"No."

She nodded. Thanks to Marcus Gold, they pretty much all had targets on their backs anyway. "Let's go." They walked out to the cars, Estanza heading to a gray Toyota, but Lucy waved him over to her Subaru.

"Thought Gold has your car bugged," he said.

"Making this a perfect time for a little conversation to perk his interest. Get in and follow my lead."

He grinned and hopped into the passenger seat. As she headed down the winding lane leading out of Fox Chapel, she started talking as if they'd been in the middle of a conversation. "Too bad that CPA refused witness protection."

"We offered," Estanza replied. "Guy might have been a financial genius as far as money laundering, but he was an idiot otherwise."

"Thank goodness my guy at the FBI is an even bigger genius when it comes to unraveling a money trail. He said he'll have the CPA's data decrypted and ready for you by the time we reach the federal building. Then we can see who was really behind the trafficking ring."

"Finally, the proof we need to nail Marcus Gold to the wall. I'll review everything and see if Graham wants to reconvene the grand jury on Monday."

Good touch, Lucy thought. "It's not only Marcus who will be going down. Everyone who got a payoff will as well. I only wish I was still with the FBI so I could be there when you take them down for the murders of Fatima and Maria."

"Don't forget the accountant. That's triple homicide in a state with the death penalty, plus federal RICO and money-laundering charges."

"And multiple counts of sex trafficking and drug smuggling. Should be enough to put them away for life whether we go with federal or state charges."

"No way out either way." He sounded so certain that even Lucy almost believed him.

They crossed the Hot Metal Bridge heading over to the South Side. Lucy shivered as they passed the spot where Alina had leaped to her death—nothing was left to mark her passing other than a ragged bouquet of dead flowers.

"You won't be able to come inside with me," Estanza told her as she pulled up to the federal building on Carson Street. His own offices in the Homeland Security building were a block away over on Sidney, but dropping him here fed into the illusion for anyone tracking Lucy's car that Estanza was going to the FBI offices. "It's a restricted area, no civilians."

"No problem. Call me when you're done, and I'll pick you up." Lucy pulled to a stop, and Estanza got out. She continued west to the shops and restaurants bustling with weekend activity and pulled into the public parking garage. From there, she walked down to the Riverfront Park and found a spot on the amphitheater steps that was out of earshot of anyone.

She dialed Nick's new burner phone. "How's it going?"

"Megan and Oshiro are having a blast, as predicted. Like this is some kind of vacation." He didn't volunteer details of their exact location—better for everyone if she didn't know.

"While you and June are doing enough worrying for everyone," she said. "I'm sorry."

"Not your fault," he said, even though they both knew it was. If she had any other job... But then she wouldn't be the woman he loved. They'd had the conversation many times during their marriage, starting when she'd gotten pregnant with Megan.

"Still, I'm sorry."

"Everything okay there?"

"Quiet. Not in a good way. More in a I'm-missing-something-obvious way."

"Ahh...okay, walk me through it."

This time, with the immediate threat to her family mitigated, Lucy gave him all the details of the case. "The thing is," she finished, "I can't reconcile the methodology with the idea of Gold as our actor. Yeah, he's arrogant, narcissistic, ruthless, and I can totally see him needing to dominate these women he feels have done him wrong, but..."

"But?"

She struggled to put her intuitions into words.

"But it's how he does it that makes no sense. The first two women were strangers to him. They were eliminated to silence their testimony and perhaps to assure his cartel partners that a message was sent to anyone else considering testifying. So the way they were tortured makes sense, but then, why give them opioids? Enough that they would have felt no pain. And then also a drug to make them forget everything—administered right before they were killed, since it was still in their system?"

"A paradox," Nick said. "Two different motivations."

"Two different psychologies? Two actors, not one?"

"Why not? These crimes sound very time intensive. Took a lot of planning and logistics given that the victims were taken from one place, kept for several days, and then moved again to a separate dump site. Plus, the thorough forensic cleanup."

"One man plans and executes the abductions, cleanup, and final dumping. And the other—the other is all about rage and dominance. He's the alpha. Dominating and controlling not just the women but his partner."

"I'd say one's the brains and one's the brawn, but I think that's oversimplifying the type of relationship you'd need for crimes like these. Both would need to be highly functional, intelligent, socially adaptable. But beneath that facade, one will be fighting low self-esteem, resentment, even fury at the more domineering partner."

"Then why not turn on the dominant partner? Why keep doing what he wants?"

Nick's shrug was almost audible as she imagined the wry expression on his face. "That's the key to breaking them. Eliminate whatever hold the alpha has over his partner, and they'll turn on each other."

"Gold must be the alpha. That's why all the victims have ties to him. But I still don't understand the first two victims."

"Maybe Gold chose them, but didn't actually participate?" Nick suggested.

"Some kind of initiation? A test to see how far Gold could control the partner." She nodded to herself. "And it would give Gold a hold over the partner."

"Never underestimate the power of a little blackmail. But that would also cause a simmering resentment in the submissive partner. I wouldn't be surprised if he didn't purposefully sabotage the alpha, a passive-aggressive act of rebellion, even though it could cost them both."

Lucy thought about that for a moment. What he described, that kind of psychology—it sounded like that silly fraternity Hunt had told her about and the way Gold had extorted his way into power there. "Would someone as egocentric as Marcus Gold choose someone weak to partner with? Or would he choose someone almost as smart and powerful as himself?"

She thought she knew the answer—she had no proof, but something felt right about it—but she waited for Nick's confirmation.

"The closer the partner is to Gold's own social level and intelligence, the greater the challenge in dominating him."

"And the greater the pleasure when he forces the partner to submit."

"Exactly. A man like Gold isn't going to shy away from a challenge like that. He'd relish it. In a way, it'd be more satisfying than getting away with the actual crimes."

"So if we break the hold Gold has on his partner, the partner should turn on him. But how do I break Gold? Make him do something reckless, hopefully in public? He's hosting a big charity gala tonight. Seems like the perfect opportunity to force his hand."

Nick thought for a moment. "Humiliation is always powerful, especially in public. But I'm not sure it would get the results you want. Instead of a public confession, he might simply double down on eliminating every possible threat." He didn't have to tell her that if she challenged Gold in public and the ploy failed, she'd be the first threat he'd target.

Lucy stood, the afternoon sun glinting from the river before her. She glanced up at the bridge overhead—the same bridge Alina had hurled herself from a few days ago. "Right. So I need to break them both."

"Do you know who the partner is?"

"I have a pretty good idea." But how to force that person to turn on Gold? Then she realized that she already had the answer. Excited, she focused on the bridge, seeking out the spot where Alina had leaped to her death. Not suicide—Hart had been right about that. Alina had killed herself to protect her child.

"I'm going to nail these bastards," she told Nick, for the first time feeling as if she was on solid ground with this case.

It was more than a promise to herself, it was a promise to Alina and all the victims.

If only she had a clue how to keep it.

Chapter 29

After everyone left, Cassie helped Rebekah clean up the lunch dishes. "This house is so big," she said as she stacked the dishwasher. "How do you manage without help?"

"We had a housekeeper and cook." Rebekah packaged the leftover chili. "Before the baby. But now, I just want it to be us. Our little family. So we let them go."

"Is that why you stopped using the night nanny as well?" Cassie couldn't imagine having strangers living in her house, but she and Drake had only the loft, so maybe with enough space it wasn't an issue.

"The baby was growing too attached to her." Rebekah's tone turned sharp. "She had to go."

"I'm sure we're not helping. Having all of us descend on you like a horde."

"Are you kidding?" She laughed. "It's the most I've seen of Graham in months. Usually, it's just him and Jared holed up in his war room—his term, not mine—squinting at their satellite surveillance or poring over interview transcripts."

They worked in silence for a few minutes, then Cassie asked, "I saw Graham's campaign posters. Running for Senate—won't that take him away from you and the baby?"

"It's something he's wanted for years. He was going to run years ago, before the car crash, but then... It's what he wants and his parents and mine. The man's a natural-born leader." She shrugged. "I'll be fine. As long as I have Jakob. Speaking of which, he'll be up soon." She took a can of formula and began prepping a bottle.

"When you went to the ad agency for Graham's campaign materials, did you meet a girl named Alina? She works for the same ad agency. Or she used to."

"Alina? No. But I was only there the one time. Graham was in several times for headshots and a few short videos. He might have met her."

The house phone rang just as the baby began to stir on the video monitor. "I'll feed the baby, if you want," Cassie volunteered. She couldn't wait to cuddle Jakob again, despite the yearning emptiness she felt when she had to give him back.

"Thanks." Rebekah handed her the bottle. "Fair warning, he'll need changing as well."

"No problem. I've got it." Cassie took the bottle and grabbed a burp cloth from the stack near the monitor, then went upstairs to the nursery.

These back steps were obviously used by the family on a daily basis. Instead of the original artwork that graced the formal main staircase, this area featured a gathering of snapshots chronicling Graham and Rebekah's life together. Their engagement photo, the obligatory cake-smearing wedding shot, the two of them goofing around in snorkel gear on the rocky beach of an azure-blue sea. Graham leering into the camera, dangling a writhing octopus as Rebekah shrieked in mock horror.

She stopped. Stepped back down to examine that one more closely. Graham had a tattoo of a G shaped like a snake on the inside of his wrist. The same tattoo Tandi Jefferson had described. The same one she said Marcus Gold had. They'd both belonged to the same fraternity.

The baby cried again, and Cassie hurried up the steps. She took the shortcut through the nanny's room into the nursery. As soon as she reached the bassinet, the baby stopped fussing.

"You stinker you," she cooed at him. "You just wanted company, didn't you? I've only been here a day, and you have me well trained already." She scooped him up. He didn't smell like he needed his diaper changed, so she sat down with him in the rocker and tried the bottle. At first, he seemed more interested in her than eating, but after a few attempts, he began to suck and slurp with contentment.

Even as she smiled down on him, tears pricked the back of her eyes. What she and Drake had lost. What Alina had lost. And yet, it was impossible to be sad for long, not while holding this joyous promise of the future in her arms.

As the baby drank, Cassie scrolled through her

phone with her other hand, curious to see exactly how well Graham knew Marcus Gold. Graham's social media presence was subdued—fitting for a US attorney and a man prepping a run for Senate. Rebekah's was a different story. Tons of photos—charity events, lunches out with friends, a variety of different yoga classes as she and her friends went on a quest to try every yoga studio in the city.

Cassie sped through the photo feed of bored rich women in their hundred-dollar leggings and sports bras. But then she stopped. The stream was in chronological order, and she was already up to August. She kept scrolling. September. October. Last week.

Rebekah didn't look pregnant in any of the photos. Cassie glanced down at the baby now asleep in her arms. She was being paranoid. Letting her imagination run wild.

She thought about it. Rebekah had mentioned the car crash, losing her first baby. Maybe she'd had an emergency hysterectomy to stop the bleeding? Jakob definitely looked like Graham—same dimple, same cleft in his chin, both hereditary traits.

In vitro. With a surrogate. That was the logical explanation. Nothing sinister about it.

She went back to rocking, chiding herself for being so desperate to keep her promise to Alina that she was suspicious of everyone, even the man who'd devoted himself to destroying Marcus Gold, to bringing him to justice. The warmth of the baby had her head nodding. Where did that baby smell come from? It made the rest of the world feel blurred and far, far away.

No way could Alina have been kept prisoner here for three months, have her baby, and then somehow escape and make it all the way into the city to the Hot Metal Bridge... It was preposterous. There was no way the Hunts could have kept all that a secret. And why would they? They were rich—if they wanted to have a baby, they could just hire a surrogate. Why target a rape victim?

Unless... Maybe Graham had learned that Marcus Gold was the man who'd raped Alina? Maybe when he found out she was pregnant, he'd offered protection, a place to deliver her baby and keep him safe while he built his case against Marcus?

If so, then why had Alina run away? Why had she been naked and alone out on that bridge? Why was she dead?

As her eyes closed and her chin nodded down, she knew she was missing something, a niggling idea that conjured a vision of Marcus Gold, Rebekah, and Graham Hunt all waltzing together in a grand ballroom. Music was playing as they moved over an intricate marble mosaic of a snake with an apple in its mouth. Rebekah swirled from one man to the other, her smile blazing in the light of the chandelier.

The trio was so beautiful, graceful, that Cassie almost missed the lone figure hiding in the shadows beyond them. Alina. Naked, hair straggling down over her shoulders, expression haunted as she stretched her arms out, pleaded voicelessly to Cassie.

Then she vanished into the darkness.

CHAPTER 30

Lucy walked along the path beside the river, reviewing her theory, trying to find any holes in it. It held up just fine. Only one problem—no hard evidence.

Her phone buzzed. Estanza. "What did you find?" she asked.

"More than I wanted." He sounded out of breath. "I still can't—"

"It was Hunt." It was the only way this all made sense. Gold's partner was the man in charge of the investigation against him. Hunt could make sure any grand jury failed to indict, making him look bold in even bringing the case, while letting Gold get away with murder, among other heinous crimes.

"Yeah. According to the database, ICE picked up both your witnesses and Alina Dolya and released them into the custody of the US Attorney's Office. To place in special protection prior to testifying. Locations classified. Files sealed." He made a small, primal sound deep in his throat. "He watched. I stood there with him as he watched them grab Alina."

"He couldn't risk the DNA test going forward on her baby. I'm not positive, but the baby might be his."

"Wait. He's not just working for Gold, he's participating in the crimes?"

As she turned and strode toward the parking garage where she'd left her car, she told him about her theory of two perpetrators and Nick's curbside psychological assessment of their relationship.

"Son of a bitch," he muttered. "He used me. Did Marcus Gold even have anything to do with the massacre of my team? Hunt's the one who told me the IP address of the drone video was traced to Gold."

"I don't know."

"Why? Why did Hunt ask me to work with him, to investigate Gold if Hunt's involved?"

"Two reasons. He hoped you'd find proof that could bring Gold down—evidence of crimes that Hunt hasn't been involved in. That's why he told you those witnesses were deported—"

"The witnesses Hunt killed. God, I was so stupid."

"That's why he didn't have you working on the trafficking case."

"The case that he was sabotaging to protect Gold—and himself," he said. "What's the second reason?"

She hesitated. "It's just a guess. To set you up as a fall guy."

He was silent for a long time. "Because of my history with the Zapatas. He'd pin those murders on me, say I was working for the cartel. But the only way that would work would be—"

"If he also implicated you in the murders of your squad."

"I betrayed my own team? Led them into that ambush?" His rage simmered through his voice. "The only way anyone would ever believe that would be if I killed myself and left a deathbed confession. Hunt could do that. He knows how to lay a money trail, could plant my DNA. And if I was dead, there'd be no real investigation, no trial."

Lucy crossed the plaza in front of the Cheesecake Factory, holding her phone close to her ear so none of the weekend shoppers could overhear. Estanza remained silent for a long time. "Jared. You okay? We don't know for sure that that's what Hunt is planning."

"No. But it fits. It's what I'd do in his shoes if I thought the net was closing in. After what he did to those two women, what's setting up a friend for a fake suicide, right?"

"I think Hunt's feeling the pressure—has been ever since Gold forced him to kill Fatima and Maria. Which means we can break him, force him to give up Gold."

"How? So he lied to ICE about the witnesses—he can say it was for the case, but they refused to cooperate, left his protective custody, whatever. We have no actual proof—" He paused. "Oh. The girl who killed herself. The last girl."

"Alina." Lucy waited for him to fill in the rest of

the blanks.

"If the baby is his—Hunt's baby? Then his wife? Rebekah's involved? She loves that baby. I thought he was theirs—she said they used IVF, a surrogate. Worse, she thinks he is her baby. She'll never let that baby go."

"Which is what we use as our leverage against Hunt." A lot depended on exactly how complicit Rebekah was. Did she know about Alina's rape? After Hunt had Alina kidnapped at the courthouse, he would have needed a secure location, someone to care for Alina during the last few months of her pregnancy, a doctor or midwife to deliver the baby and give him a legitimate birth certificate. Hunt had the resources to do all that—but what did Rebekah know about where her baby came from? "We need to be careful. Threatening a man's family—it could backfire."

"I don't care. We have to stop him. Them. Hunt and Gold."

"Meet me outside the federal building, the Sidney Street gate." She paid for her parking. "And remember, my car is bugged—probably audio and video. So by the time I get there, you need to calm down and put your game face on. Can you do that?"

"Yeah." He bit out the word in a grudging tone.

"I'm on my way."

Chapter 31

Cassie woke to find the baby squirming because of a wet diaper. She wiped the drool from her chin and blinked. She hadn't had a nice, long nap like that in ages. She moved the baby over to his changing table and quickly took care of the diaper. He made a soft noise of contentment and went right back to sleep.

She lay him in his crib and went to wash her hands in the bathroom that connected the nursery to the nanny's room. The sky-blue nautical theme extended here, but when she glanced through to the nanny's room, she saw that any attempt at decoration ended. The walls were bare, a twin bed stripped down to the mattress was pushed against the far corner, and the dresser was plain white, no mirror. Given the abundance of personality that the rest of the house exuded, it felt strange.

Cassie sighed as she glanced in the mirror above the sink. She hadn't really slept since Alina's death, and it showed. She'd hit the stage of exhaustion where there was a constant buzz in her head accompanying a throbbing pain that was certain to soon explode. Hoping to find a pain reliever, she opened the medicine cabinet. The shelves were bare.

Stuck to the back of the mirrored door was a printout from a fetal ultrasound. Its edges were worn, as if someone had repeatedly handled it. Cassie squinted at the tiny white print in the corner that identified the mother and the date of the test.

Alina Dolya. Her last visit before she'd been abducted.

Cassie gasped. Alina had been here!

She reached to grab the ultrasound, but then stopped. Never touch evidence until it's documented. That's what Drake shouted at all the TV cops who blithely picked up clues hither and yon. She used her phone to take photos of the bathroom, the back of the mirror with the ultrasound, then close-ups of the image, showing Alina's name and the date. Her hands trembled, so she had to take several shots before she got one that wasn't blurred. Why was Alina—

Jakob was hers. He had to be. They'd need to do DNA testing to be certain, but nothing else made sense.

But how? The US attorney didn't go around kidnapping pregnant young Ukrainians. She remembered the video Wash had found—both Graham and his investigator, Jared, at the courthouse the day Alina was taken. Were they both involved? Maybe they'd taken her into protective custody? If they were trying to hide her from someone like

Marcus Gold, maybe they had to keep it a secret, use unofficial channels, including using Graham's own residence as a safe house.

Maybe. Except, how had Alina ended up jumping off a bridge naked?

Cassie started to call Drake to ask him what she should do, even though she knew the answer. He'd tell her to go home, lock the door, and leave the police work to him. But she couldn't leave Jakob, not if he really was Alina's son.

The call wouldn't go through. For some reason, she'd lost service and she didn't have the Hunts' Wi-Fi passcode to use it. She glanced at the sleeping baby. Wouldn't hurt to have a quick look around before going downstairs and calling Drake. She started in the bathroom, searching for any other signs that Alina had been there. Nothing.

Then she moved into the nanny's room. The closet was empty except for a few empty hangers. The dresser drawers were also empty. The bedside table had only a lamp, the cheap metal kind that would be at home in any college dorm room. There was nothing tucked between the mattress and box spring, nothing fallen behind the headboard, which was solid wood, no place to hide anything.

She sat on the bed, discouraged. There was a small window, no curtains, just blinds. But other than that, the room could have been a jail cell. Maybe it had been a jail cell—not a sanctuary? No, she couldn't believe Rebekah would have any part of keeping a pregnant woman captive.

Wait. Alina delivered her baby after she'd been taken. If she'd been in protective custody, that would have required a doctor or midwife, a birth certificate, documentation. Why go through all that trouble?

Marcus Gold. It had to be. Graham was obsessed with him. If Alina's baby's DNA was the key to nailing Marcus, Graham would have done anything to build his case. Including keeping Alina a virtual prisoner—for her own safety—until she had the baby, when he could collect the evidence he needed. Far better than the fetal DNA testing Cassie and Stefi had planned—that could have been thrown out in court and would have made Alina a walking target once Marcus heard of their efforts. Which all explained taking Alina and keeping her until the baby was born...

But how had Alina ended up on that bridge?

The baby made a small noise. Cassie returned to his room. He was smiling in his sleep. She sat back down in the rocker and checked her phone again—still no bars. She paced the room, searching for any service. Maybe near the window. She pushed the blue curtains with their anchors and boats aside. One curtain felt heavier, weighted down. She felt along the hem. Definitely something in there, about the size of a nickel.

Cassie raised the opening to the hem over her palm and shook the length of the fabric until the item finally dislodged. It was a chain with a small medallion, an enameled icon. Saint Olga of Kiev, she recognized. Alina had bought it at an Easter festival, had never taken it off. Said Olga was a mother as well and would protect her baby.

Alina must have left it behind to protect her son. But there'd be no need to keep that a secret if she'd been here willingly. Cassie pocketed the medallion and glanced down at the baby. She was tempted to take him with her, but she wasn't sure what the situation really was or how dangerous. Alina might have stood here, trying to make this same decision, she realized.

She went to the door. It was locked. From the outside. Cassie ran through the bathroom into the nanny's room. That door was also locked. She checked the windows in both rooms—they were designed not to open.

Her head pounded in time with her racing pulse as she glanced around, searching for a way out, a weapon, anything.

Then Rebekah's voice came through the baby monitor near the crib. "I've been watching you on the monitors, Cassie. There's no way out."

CHAPTER 32

LUCY PICKED UP ESTANZA across from the federal building's entrance. Just as he got into the passenger seat and buckled up, her new phone vibrated inside her jacket pocket. Resisting the urge to pull it out and answer—and potentially tip their hand, given that she was certain Gold was watching and listening—she instead turned into the gas station on the corner opposite the federal building. "Got to fill up."

Estanza nodded. "Want me to pump the gas?"

She pulled up to the nearest pump. "My car. I can manage filling up my gas tank, thanks."

"Sure. Just being gentlemanly."

Lucy hopped out of the car, Estanza turning on the radio to further cover her movements. She opened the gas cap, put the nozzle in, but didn't actually activate the pump. Instead, she pretended the credit card reader wasn't working and headed toward the store. Before going inside, she ducked behind a large pickup and headed to the far side of the building where there was a concrete block wall demarcating the air pump area. No one was within hearing distance, and no one could see her behind the wall, but she had a good angle to keep an eye on her car. She slid her phone free. The missed call came from Drake. He and Carter had been investigating the CPA's movements before his death. She called him back.

"Hey," he answered. "We got something. The CPA was actually pretty smart, covering his tracks, but he met with his attorney before he was scheduled to testify."

"At the law office?"

"No. The attorney said the guy was paranoid, so they met at a little coffee shop—right around the corner from where the CPA died."

"They followed the lawyer, not the CPA."

"Exactly. We got video from the café. There were two of them. Girls, college age. One bumps into the lawyer, drops her muffin—"

"Scone." Carter's voice came through, correcting him.

"Scone. Whatever. Both the lawyer and our guy are distracted—"

"While the other girl doses him," Lucy finished. "Any IDs on our actors?" Or actresses. Seemed killing for hire was an equal-opportunity profession.

"Working on it. Anything from your end?"

She hesitated, gauging how they'd react, but then remembered that Drake's wife was still at Hunt's house. "Yeah. But I need you to think before you act."

"Why?"

"Because we think Graham Hunt's involved.

Working with Gold. Estanza found evidence that he covered up my two witnesses' murders and helped arrange Alina's kidnapping."

"The hell. Hart's still there."

"She was right. The baby's the key. It's either Hunt's or Gold's. We need to confront Hunt, force him to flip on Gold."

"Not until I get Hart out of there."

"Just make sure she doesn't tip our hand too soon. We're heading there now—" She stopped, movement from the federal building catching her eye. Two large black SUVs raced out of the government parking lot, but instead of turning onto Carson Street, they veered into the gas station, taking positions to block her Subaru. "Wait. Something's going on."

Men clad in tactical armor scrambled out of the vehicles, waving the other customers back from Lucy's car. "Passenger. Show us your hands. Stay in the vehicle. Show us your hands!"

They didn't swarm the car or instruct Estanza to leave it or surrender. Instead, they were containing him. Lucy recognized the tactics as those used when there was a suspected suicide bomber.

"Drake—" A blast knocked her onto her back, behind the concrete wall, followed by the sound of an explosion and a rush of air. From her position on the ground, she saw flames shoot up, filling the sky with black smoke. Screams echoed as if from far away, her hearing muffled. She still clutched the phone, could feel more than hear Drake's voice shouting at her.

She rolled over onto all fours, gasping for breath

before climbing to her feet. Car alarms filled the air. The store's windows were all blown out, glass everywhere. The metal roof over the fuel pumps was torn open where her car was, the rest of the expanse buckled and crumpled. Three agents were down, but moving, while several civilians were screaming, but no one seemed seriously injured.

Vehicles on Carson Street were stopping, people rushing to aid the injured civilians and FBI agents. Somewhere in the back of her mind, she realized that the FBI agents arrived so fast because they must have been alerted by the chemical-biological-explosive detectors that ringed the federal building.

She blinked against tears as smoke filled her eyes. Her car was a blackened, twisted hulk, flames dancing around the burnt carcass that had been a man mere seconds before. Jared Estanza. His hands were still held up high, palms turned out, elbows bent, as if he'd had no time to react. Maybe that meant he hadn't felt anything, she tried to console herself, but she knew better. Medical examiners called it the pugilistic pose, characteristic of bodies burned by high-intensity flames.

One of the agents sprinted for the store, yelling at someone inside to turn off the gas before the pumps exploded. The others pushed themselves to their feet and began directing civilians to back away from the flames, helping the wounded.

"Lucy!" Drake's voice finally reached her.

"I'm okay." Her voice was shaky. She took a breath. It tasted of gasoline. "There was a bomb. A bomb. In my car. Jared Estanza's dead." Somehow, reciting the obvious facts didn't make them feel any more real. "They blew up my car. The FBI's here."

"Get out of there," he ordered. "Lucy. Run. Now."

"But—" Shouldn't she help? Help who? Jared was dead.

"Run. They're going to think you did it. Even if they believe you're a target, they'll hold you there, asking questions for hours."

"Long enough for Hunt or Gold to find me." She darted along the wall, heading to the rear of the store. Her balance was off, one ear still ringing, but other than that she wasn't hurt. She cut behind the store, crossing a culvert into the parking lot of the commercial building beside the store. "They thought I was at the car. They wanted to kill me."

"I'm heading to Hunt's, getting Hart out of there. Where can Carter pick you up?"

Sirens blasted through the air. Lucy swallowed, her ears finally popping. She glanced around. "Heritage Park. Base of the Hot Metal Bridge."

"She'll be there in ten. Tell me what you found, any evidence we can use."

She kept moving as she told him everything, being as specific as possible in case he had to retrace her and Jared's steps. In case she was no longer around to do it herself. By the time she finished, she was standing across from the park's entrance, the Hot Metal Bridge with its intricate iron girders towering overhead, filling the sky above the river. "Drake, if something happens, tell my husband—"

"Nothing's going to happen. We're going to nail these bastards. One way or the other."

"Hart was right. Alina's baby is the key. Use him to break Hunt."

"Happily. What are you going to do?"

A car horn honked. Carter, pulling to the curb. "Carter and I are crashing Gold's party."

"No. Don't tip our hand too soon. We don't have enough evidence—"

"The man just killed Jared. Tried to kill me. He's not walking away. Not from that." Rage fueled her words. She really didn't have a plan, was propelled by blind fury.

Lucy yanked open the passenger door of Carter's Impala and dropped down into the seat. Drake was still arguing, but she hung up on him, in no mood for logic. She glanced at the clock—they had two hours before Gold's charity gala began.

If Lucy had her way, they'd be Gold's last hours as a free man.

CHAPTER 33

CASSIE POUNDED ON THE DOOR. "Rebekah, just open the door so we can talk. In person."

Silence. Followed a few moments later by heavy footsteps on the hallway's hardwood floors.

"Everything I've done," came Graham's voice, "I've done to save our family, to save us."

"You're so delusional, you actually believe that load of crap, don't you?" Rebekah's voice was shrill, easily heard through the closed door. Cassie slipped her phone free. Still no signal, but that didn't mean she couldn't record. She pressed it up to the door, holding her hand over it to hide it from the cameras.

Rebekah continued, "Why can't you get it through your head, Graham? There is no us—not since you almost killed me, not since you did kill our baby!"

"The crash wasn't my fault. It was Marcus—"

"Marcus had nothing to do with the crash. It was you, Graham. All you. You murdered our baby."

"If you hadn't been flirting with Marcus, practically crawling all over him, I wouldn't have drunk so much—"

"So now it's my fault?" Rebekah shot back. "Funny how it always comes back to that. My fault you killed our baby and almost killed me. My fault that I couldn't have children or walk after the crash—"

"Yes! I did everything for you. Marcus said he'd give you the treatments to help you walk again if I killed those witnesses and showed the Zapata cartel they had nothing to worry about, that I'd buried their case. And I did it. For you. Even though it meant selling my soul to the devil himself, I did it. Because of what I did, you finally have a baby. I did it, I saved our family."

"Well, then, finish the job. What do we do now? She knows. I'm not losing another baby because of you, Graham. No way in hell."

Their voices drifted away, then returned once more. There was a sharp rap on the door. "Cassie, move away from the door," Graham ordered. "Go on now. I can see you on the cameras."

Cassie slid her phone, still recording, into her pocket and backed up a few steps, just far enough to give her room to maneuver. She had a brown belt in Kempo, was training for her black belt. She never wanted to resort to violence, not if there was another way, but she wasn't going to let them hurt her or Jakob.

"Pick up the baby and take a seat in the rocking chair with your back to the door," Graham continued.

No. That would leave her defenseless, impossible to strike back against any threat, not with the baby in her lap. Just as he intended.

The door opened. Graham stood, a pistol aimed at Cassie. Rebekah was right behind him, her expression anything but motherly. "Do as I say. Pick up the baby and take a seat."

There was no way he could miss her, not at this range. And even with years of Kempo training, she still couldn't outrun a bullet. She tried another tactic, playing scared and meek, obeying his orders. Hoping she could somehow find a chink in their armor, talk her way out of this. At the very least, if she was holding the baby, she could protect him.

"You did it. You kidnapped and raped those women," Cassie said in as nonjudgmental a tone as she could muster, rocking Alina's baby while Graham held a gun on them both. "You took Alina. This is her baby."

"No. Yes. I didn't rape them—that was all Marcus. He chose them, women he thought had screwed him over. Made me kidnap them, watch as he—"

"Why would he do that? Risk everything? There are easier ways to get revenge—" Cassie asked.

"He wanted more than revenge. He wanted every day for the rest of their lives to be about him, about what he did, about how he controlled whether they lived or died."

She blinked, the image of what Marcus' victims—and Hunt's victims—had suffered racing through her vision. Tried to force her anger aside. "Why involve you? Risk you talking? Marcus is smarter than that. Why would he trust you?"

Graham's face fell, his gun drifting down slightly. Not far enough for Cassie to take advantage of, not at point-blank range. But still, it was a positive sign. She was getting to him, breaching his barriers.

Then Rebekah stepped forward, her posture rigid with fury and disdain. "Because Marcus owns him. Idiot. Go on, tell her what you did."

Graham swallowed, eyed his wife, who glared right back at him, and nodded. "He filmed the first two—the women I killed. They weren't raped, I promise you. I made their deaths as humane as possible. But just killing them wasn't enough for Marcus. He said if I didn't do what he told me to, he'd stop Rebekah's treatments—or worse, he'd make sure she had a devastating side effect, like a stroke or something even worse." He turned to Rebekah. "Bekah, I couldn't risk it, couldn't lose you."

"So we're back to it being all my fault," she scoffed.

"No. Never. I'll make this right, I promise."

"How?" Rebekah asked, scorn coloring her voice. "As always, you've screwed up everything."

Cassie didn't say it, but the obvious answer was to eliminate the threat: her. But no, given that Lucy, Stefi, and Drake were on the case, not to mention the others at Beacon Falls, Hunt really had no options left. She just needed to make him see that. "Why don't you give yourself up?" she suggested. "At least that way, your family would be protected."

"But I'd lose everything. Marcus would make

certain of that. He'd release the videos, humiliate me in public."

As if the women he'd killed didn't matter. Only his pride. Cassie tried again. "At least tell me what happened to Alina. What really happened. Why did Marcus target her?"

"Alina." Her name was a plaintive sigh. But he didn't address his words to Cassie. Rather, he turned to Rebekah. "After the wreck, you grew so cold, distant. I thought I'd never feel anything for another woman. It was like I was empty. But then she was there—at the ad agency when we went to film that campaign commercial. She was so kind and thoughtful. She listened…"

"That's why you went back for new headshots—twice," Rebekah said. "To see her."

"I didn't touch her, I promise you. We just talked. I showed her the city. It was like seeing everything again for the first time. She made me laugh. I felt like a kid—like I did when you and I were dating."

Rebekah stalked across the room to the window, her back to her husband and Cassie.

"I wanted to take things further, tried to kiss her." Graham focused on Cassie, pleading with her to understand, as if she were the jury and he was on trial. "She—she said no, I was married, she didn't love me, not like that. I grabbed her, and this fury, this white-hot rage, it just came over me. I thought of what Marcus did to those others, what I wanted to do to him, how I wanted him to suffer. Then I blinked, and it wasn't Marcus, it was Alina. Dear, sweet, innocent Alina, bleeding and bruised, looking at me like I was a monster. So I used the drug Marcus gave me, dumped her like all the others. But then..."

"You found out she was pregnant. And that we could use the baby's DNA against you."

"At first, I panicked. But then I realized it was a blessing from God. I could finally give Rebekah everything she wanted. Make up for everything I've done. It was our chance to start over."

Rebekah whirled at that. "Our?" she mocked. "No, Graham. This is all on you. For once in your life, be a man. Take care of Marcus, once and for all. Finish this. Now. Tonight. It's the only way to save our family." She held his gaze, her expression softening. "I can't live if they take Jakob from me. I can lose everything else, but not him."

Cassie forced herself to remain quiet. Rebekah was delusional if she thought she could somehow keep Jakob if Graham confessed. Although, maybe legally, she could—but only if Graham exonerated Rebekah of any involvement in Alina's kidnapping. If he lied for her, sacrificed himself.

Rebekah and Graham were silent, but his shoulders squared as if he were accepting her challenge. He crossed the room, bending over to kiss Jakob on his head, ignoring Cassie as if she weren't even there, then handed Rebekah the pistol and kissed her as well. "Leave it to me," he said. "No one will touch you or Jakob. You'll never need to worry about Marcus Gold again."

He left without a backward glance. Cassie stirred, hoping that Rebekah would let her go, but the other woman held the pistol just as confidently as her husband had. "No," she said. "You stay right where you are. Graham is an idiot, but as long as he keeps me out of it, we'll be fine." She focused on the baby in Cassie's arms, and her tone turned singsong. "Won't we, Jakob? We'll be so happy. Just the two of us."

Chapter 34

"You're in shock," Carter told Lucy as they drove over the bridge and into Oakland. "I should get you to the hospital."

Lucy shook her head, regretting the movement as it turned up the volume of the throbbing behind her eyes. "I'm fine. Just find a quiet place where we can think."

Carter turned onto Greenfield, and they headed into Schenley Park, cruising the winding roads until they found a secluded parking lot near the running trails. They were the only car, and given that the sun was about to set, there was no one to be seen on the trail either. Lucy sat, the quiet surrounding the car dampening the chaos inside her mind. Every time she blinked, she saw Jared's body, tasted ash and burning gasoline.

"I need to call Nick. In case he hears something on the news." She held her phone, but couldn't bring herself to dial, the churning in her gut sending bile clawing up her throat. She swallowed, clamping her jaw shut against the urge to vomit.

Carter got out of her seat and opened the trunk. She returned with a small cooler bag. "Emergency rations. Drink this." She handed Lucy an electrolyte drink. Lucy's hands trembled so badly that she couldn't manage the twist-off cap. Carter took care of that as well. Lucy sipped at the drink, not even tasting it over the acrid burning that filled her throat. But it did its job, stilling the rebellion in her stomach, calming the adrenaline-fueled jitters that shook her muscles.

She dialed Nick. "I'm okay," she started.

"Why wouldn't you be?" he asked, an edge to his voice. He'd gotten far too many calls like this over the years; it was one of the reasons why she'd left the FBI behind. Somehow, that hadn't helped matters—danger still found her. "What happened?"

She gave him an abbreviated and severely edited version of events. "I'm fine. But Estanza's dead, and they think I am, too. Didn't want you to worry in case anyone called, or if it was on the news."

"There was a bomb." His words were slow, still digesting what happened. "In your car. And it went off."

"I'm fine," she repeated. "I was nowhere near—"

"It was your car, Lucy! You should have been, they thought you were—"

"But I wasn't." Why were they arguing over the fact that she'd just escaped a particularly gruesome demise?

"You're coming to join us." It wasn't a question.

"No. I can't."

"If they think you're dead, let them keep thinking it," he said. "They won't be hunting for you."

"They will as soon as they don't find my body in the wreckage. Which won't take them long. I can't put you and Megan in danger. I won't," she added, forestalling any further debate.

"Fine. But you need to go into hiding. I'll send Oshiro—"

"No. Nick." Her voice ratcheted tight with fury. "These men, they've destroyed seven women's lives just for the hell of it. They killed Estanza, would have killed me, because we're just meaningless pawns in their pissing match. They're rich and powerful, and they think they can get away with anything. This needs to end. Now."

"Yeah, but why do you need to be the one to end it? Why can't you leave it to the police or Homeland or the FBI? Why you, Lucy?"

Because a good man was just burned alive in her car while she watched, she wanted to scream. She swallowed the words and softened her tone. "I love you."

"Doesn't answer my question," he snapped.

"Everything is going to be okay. You and Megan will be safe, can come home. Just give me a little more time. I promise."

"Promise what? That you'll be safe and waiting at home when we get there? Promise me that, Lucy. Don't give me vague reassurances or tell me that you'll take care of Marcus Gold and Hunt. I don't care about them. I care about you. I want you home, safe. Or somewhere, anywhere. Safe. Now."

She glanced at Carter, who sat very still, trying to pretend that she couldn't hear every word. "I have to go. I love you."

She hung up as tears ambushed her. It wasn't fair. Not to Nick, not to Megan. But she had to see this through—a man had died because of her. It was more than duty or honor or even a passion for justice. It was a debt that she might never repay. But she had to try.

Finally, she blew her nose, used the wipe Carter handed her to clean her face, and turned to the detective. "Any ideas how we can get into Gold's party?"

"I've been thinking about that, and I think I have a plan. But we need to get you clean clothes." She grimaced at Lucy's two-day-old, smoke-stenched jeans and shirt. "Good thing we're about the same size." She went to the trunk and returned with a pair of black slacks and a plain, white shirt that appeared virtually identical to what she wore herself. "Ever work as a waitress?"

"No, but pretty sure I can fake it." Lucy took the clothing and quickly changed in the gathering shadows beside the car. No one was near, though she really didn't care about modesty at this point.

They returned to the car. "Any idea what you're going to do once we get inside? Marcus Gold might think you're dead, but that's not enough to rattle a man like him. He'll have his own security, and the police will be looking for you, want some answers about that car bomb. Hate to see you dragged off in cuffs."

Lucy rolled her eyes as she turned up the hem on Carter's slacks. "Been there, done that. Not about to let it happen again. No. I'm thinking something much more public and personal. What's the main problem you face with sexual assaults?"

"Getting the victims to disclose. Over eighty percent never report, and those that do, often can't bring themselves to testify. They know the defense will put them on trial, try to eviscerate them. It's like being raped all over again, only this time in public for everyone to see."

"So let's use our victims' own words. Put Gold on trial. In full view of the public."

Carter's eyes widened. She started the car's engine. "It might work. And if not, I'll ask them to put me in the jail cell beside you."

CHAPTER 35

THE BABY FUSSED A BIT, and Rebekah backed away as Cassie soothed him back to sleep. Cassie watched the other woman's expression carefully. As angry and resentful as Rebekah was at Graham, she truly seemed to care about Jakob.

"It must have been hard, having Alina here," she said.

Rebekah snorted. "You have no idea. One day, I'm hosting bridge club and Graham comes in, says he has a surprise for me downstairs in the basement. I go down, and here's this girl, this very, very pregnant girl, this very, very scared girl, and Graham's strutting like a rooster, saying she's going to be our surrogate and we're going to be a family."

"Wow. Did Alina understand any of it?"

"Poor thing. Graham had her convinced this was all part of her testifying, like we were some kind of witness protection. At first. Took me weeks to finally get the truth from him and her just about as long to realize what was really happening." She jerked her chin at the door. "Don't believe that fairy tale he just spun about how they had some kind of love at first sight. He stalked the girl. Spied on her, sent her little gifts and notes, popped up wherever she was, until he finally convinced her—or, more likely, she felt like her job might be threatened if she said no—to go out for coffee with him. Poor kid, she was just being polite, trying to save her job, stay in the country. She never felt anything for him. It was all in his imagination."

Cassie noted the sympathy that had crept into her voice. She could use that, she hoped. "How did she end up on that bridge? Did you help her escape, but something went wrong?"

Rebekah's gaze sharpened. She considered Cassie for a few moments before answering. "I could spin you a lie, but it wouldn't matter. It was me."

"You?"

"Alina loved Jakob—as much as I did. As I do. She took care of Jakob at night, but I could tell, when I'd come get him for his morning feedings, he was growing attached to her. Then one night, I caught Graham coming out of her room. He swore he was in there to check on the baby, change his diaper." She scoffed. "As if the man ever lifted a finger to help with anything. I checked the security footage, and he'd been watching Alina while she was sleeping. Didn't touch her, just stood there, watching her. Then he started dropping hints about keeping her, as if she was his pet. Said things like I had Jakob, why shouldn't he have someone to take care of?"

Cassie could see where this was going. Rebekah

might be less delusional than Graham, but she was just as dangerous. "So you had to get rid of her," she said in a low tone, holding the baby tighter, as if she could protect him from the truth.

"If she'd stayed, sooner or later someone would have seen her, or she would have escaped, told. And then I'd lose the baby. So, yes, she had to go."

"Why make her kill herself?"

"Graham would've been impossible to live with if he thought I'd killed her. So I used that drug Marcus gave him. Graham told me that a low dose makes people do whatever you tell them to, so one night I put a sleeping pill in his nightcap, woke Alina, gave her the drug, and drove her out to the bridge. I wasn't sure what forensics could do with her clothes—we were the same size, so she wore old stuff I had. I made her strip, told her if she didn't jump, the baby would die, put the fear of God in her. I think maybe, after everything she'd been through, I probably didn't even need to use the drug. But maybe it eased her way. I hope."

Cassie just stared at the woman. "You know she'd only just turned nineteen."

"Yeah. I made her a birthday cake." She shook her head at the memory. "Funny thing. Different circumstances, without Graham screwing things up, I think we could have been friends. Could have loved Jakob together, raised him up to be a good man, nothing like his father." Her gaze settled on the baby in Cassie's arms.

That's when Cassie realized that holding Jakob

was her edge. She pushed out of the rocker and stood. Rebekah startled, raising the pistol. "You're not going to shoot. You won't risk hurting Jakob." She took a step toward Rebekah and held out a hand. "Give me the gun, Rebekah."

Rebekah hesitated, but then came the sound of a man's voice shouting Cassie's name from downstairs. Drake. Perfect timing.

"It's over," Cassie said in a soft tone. "Give me the gun."

Tears streamed down Rebekah's face as she handed the pistol to Cassie. Footsteps thundered down the hallway, and Drake rushed into the room. "Hart. You okay?"

Cassie kept her eyes on Rebekah. "We're fine. Everything's fine."

Chapter 36

THEY STOPPED AT A DINER with free Wi-Fi. While Carter connected with Wash at Beacon Falls, Lucy used the restroom to wash up more thoroughly and make herself look presentable and forgettable. Powdery glass fragments were caught in her hair. She finger-combed it as best she could, then pulled it back into a businesslike ponytail.

By the time Drake called with an update on Hart, she and Carter had their plan mapped out. It helped that Gold's penthouse on Mount Washington had been featured in numerous architectural magazines, allowing them to get the lay of the land. But then they listened to Hunt's confession that Hart had recorded, and everything changed. Finally, they had a weapon that Gold would be forced to respond to: his partner's confession.

"Downside is," Drake told them, "Hunt's gone to confront Gold on his own. At least that's what he told his wife. He's going to be a wildcard."

"We should consider him armed and

dangerous," Lucy said as she and Carter huddled in a booth over the phone, listening with the volume as low as possible.

"Doesn't help that a BOLO on you just went live," Carter said, reading from her laptop. "Person of interest in possible terrorist attack. Approach with caution. It's hitting all the news outlets. Terrible picture, but it's you."

"Lucy, you should sit this out," Drake said. "I'll go in with Carter."

"With Hunt having a head start, I don't think we can wait for you to get here. But if you have any pull with the brass—someone you trust not to tip off Gold or Hunt—might help protect Carter and me from any trigger-happy patrolmen."

"Already alerted my commander, and she sent a team to take custody of Hunt's wife. Not too happy about the multijurisdictional political entanglements, but she'll help out. What about the feds?"

"I'll call my old boss," Lucy told him. "But not sure who he can trust over there. Or who will believe him. Hunt is well respected, and with a federal agent getting blown up, tempers will be high."

Drake made a grunting noise of acknowledgment. Carter snapped her laptop shut. "Wash has everything set. Time to go."

"I'll get there as soon as possible," Drake said. "In the meantime, be careful."

The gala was already underway by the time they arrived. Lucy waited at the kitchen entrance to Gold's penthouse, with its sweeping million-dollar views of the Point and downtown, while Carter used her badge to gain admission on the pretext of a security check, given the car bombing. A few minutes later, she opened the service door to let Lucy in. The staff of caterers was busy with their work. No one even questioned their presence.

The hardest part was that they'd decided Lucy should be unarmed. She was no longer law enforcement, and if she drew a weapon—especially now that news was out that she was wanted for questioning in a possible terrorist attack—things could turn ugly very, very fast. Lucy understood Carter's reasons, but it didn't help her feel less naked, walking into the lair of a beast like Gold without a weapon.

They left the kitchen and entered the ballroom where the guests were mingling, bidding on silent auction items—some of which cost more than Lucy's house. A podium set up in front of the head table had a projection screen behind it, filling the wall. They'd timed it perfectly, thanks to the event program Carter had found. Marcus Gold was making his way through the room, shaking hands, heading to the podium as servers circulated with trays of champagne for a predinner toast. A local TV news crew followed him, filming everything.

As Gold reached the podium, a waitress stepped out of the shadows to greet him with a full flute of champagne. He took it and turned to address the crowd, mouthing platitudes that Lucy ignored.

"Does she look familiar?" Lucy asked as the waitress retreated to stand in the far corner behind him. "I think—"

"That's Tandi Jefferson," Carter said.

"What the hell is she doing here?"

"I'm not sure. I thought she was pretty much agoraphobic. Why—" Gold drank the champagne and gestured to Tandi, who rushed over with another flute. Carter answered her own question. "Did we just witness her drug Marcus Gold?"

"I can't believe he didn't even look at her, much less recognize her."

"Arrogant bastard." Carter's bitter tone surprised Lucy. "Probably wouldn't remember who she was if he did look at her."

Lucy kept her back to the wall as she moved to get a better angle, Carter following. "I don't like the way she has her hand in the pocket of her apron. I think she's armed."

"We should stop this."

"Wait. Let Wash do his thing, distract everyone. That way, we can get close to her, take her down if we need to. Otherwise, we risk civilians getting hurt." As they sidled nearer to Tandi, the irony wasn't lost on Lucy—if Tandi was here to kill Gold, then she and Carter were about to save his life.

Then the lights dimmed as Gold spoke about the charity's end-of-year accomplishments. But instead of the originally programmed slide show, a very different show began.

Carter and Wash had figured they had, at most, fifteen to twenty seconds before Gold's people shut down the projector—the only weakness in Gold's cybersecurity since the projector had its own internet connection—so Wash had edited the material to be as dramatic as possible as quickly as possible.

Slides of Gold's victims, before and after, filled the wall behind him. At first, he had no clue why his audience was gasping in horror. Then Hunt's voice began. "I didn't rape them—that was Marcus. He chose them, women he thought had screwed him over. He wanted more than revenge. He wanted every day for the rest of their lives to be about him, about what he did, about how he controlled whether they lived or died."

"Cut it off!" Gold shouted toward the projection booth at the other end of the room. Then the room went black as the projector went dead. People instinctively crowded together, murmuring. When the lights came on, everyone looked at one another—anywhere but at their host.

Except for the TV crew filming everything. The reporter, a tall blonde in a powder-blue formal gown, stepped toward Gold, brandishing her microphone. "Care to comment, Mr. Gold?"

Gold whirled on her, fire in his eyes. "I don't comment on lies. The man you just heard, he's the real criminal. Graham Hunt. He has a vendetta against me. You can't believe anything the man says."

"Graham Hunt, the US attorney?" the reporter asked, but Gold ignored her. He turned back to scan the crowd. Despite it not being part of their script, Lucy stepped forward, catching his attention. And, more important, Tandi's, allowing Carter to get closer to the potential assassin.

Gold motioned to his security staff. "Get them the hell out. Get everyone the hell out of here. Now!"

Reluctantly, the crowd let themselves be shepherded out until the cavernous room was vacant except for Gold, Carter, Lucy, and—still hiding in the shadows behind Gold—Tandi Jefferson.

"You're a difficult woman to kill, Lucy," he sneered as she approached. He clutched the podium with both hands—an effect of the drug Tandi might have used in the champagne? Or a reflection of his rage?

The sound of the main doors being shut echoed through the tall-ceilinged space. Gold's expression morphed to one of triumph. "Graham. Knew you had to be behind all this."

Lucy glanced over her shoulder. Graham Hunt was locking the door behind him—Gold's security on the other side. He wore a tuxedo, but somehow it hung on him, as if he'd lost weight in the hours since she'd seen him last. When he turned around, he drew a pistol from his jacket. His eyes were wide, focused only on Gold. "Game's over, Marcus!"

"And you lose," Gold called back. He turned his attention on Lucy, who stood between him and Hunt. "You all lose. But I'll give you one last chance to save yourself, Lucy. Kill him and save me, the man who's going to save the planet and the entire human race. Kill him, and I'll make you a hero." He jerked his chin toward Hunt. "After all, the only real evidence points to Graham. Do it for the greater good, Lucy. Let me walk away. I'll see that you're richly rewarded."

Hunt crossed the room. Now only a dozen feet separated him and Gold, with Lucy caught in no man's land. "Lucy knows how many convictions will be overturned if I take the fall for you, Marcus. She'll never let all those rapists and pedophiles, killers, corrupt officials, domestic terrorists go free." He glanced at Carter, obviously not seeing Tandi as a threat. "Arrest him, Detective. It's time the great Marcus Gold finally pays for his crimes."

Carter appeared torn. She was almost within striking distance of Tandi, but now her cover was blown. Before Carter could act, Tandi pulled a compact semiautomatic from her apron. Instead of taking aim at Gold, she whirled on Hunt, firing twice before Carter could grab her. Lucy rushed Hunt, tackling him as he returned fire, his aim wide, the bullets dislodging plaster from the ceiling above them. They fell to the floor, Lucy on top.

"No," he screamed, his voice high-pitched as they grappled for his gun. "He wants to take my family! I have to stop him."

Lucy didn't waste breath on words, instead aimed a well-placed knee to Hunt's groin, followed by a punch to his solar plexus. Hunt's breath whooshed out, and he crumbled in pain, allowing her to wrest his pistol from him.

Holding the weapon, still crouched over Hunt, she spun to see that Carter had Tandi face down on the floor and was handcuffing her wrists behind her. Gold was curled up behind the podium. Lucy turned back to Hunt, opening the flaps of his jacket to check him for more weapons. Then she saw the blood blossoming from a wound at the bottom of his rib cage. Right over his liver.

Hunt stared at her, his breath coming fast and shallow. She applied pressure, using her hands and her body weight. With all the blood vessels near the liver, she wasn't sure if she was doing more harm than good. "Get help!"

Carter scrambled to her feet and ran to unlock the doors. Hunt's face turned ashen, his lips quivering. He grabbed Lucy's wrist, pulling her down. "Tell Bekah," he gasped. "All for her."

Then he went limp.

Behind her, Tandi laughed. Lucy glanced over her shoulder as Tandi rolled over and awkwardly pushed herself to a sitting position. "Got them," she said, her tone triumphant. "Got 'em both. Bastards. Thought they were untouchable."

Gold's security guards rushed in, two of them taking over for Lucy, while two more ran to Gold, slumped on the floor near the podium. "Boss? Mr. Gold?"

"Gave him a dose of his own medicine. He's gone," Tandi told them, her smile ghastly. "And he's never coming back."

CHAPTER 37

THE NEXT DAY, Lucy waited impatiently at Beacon Falls, pacing up and down the drive until finally she spotted a beat-up Dodge Caravan approaching. She ran up to it as it pulled to a stop, Oshiro waving from the driver's seat, Megan leaping out of the back, and Nick climbing down from the passenger's side.

She hugged her family, ignoring Nick's raised eyebrow promising a long, long discussion to follow, and turned to Oshiro. "This is the vehicle you trusted my family's life to?"

"Blends in anywhere. If the bad guys can't spot you, there's no need for speed. Although, this baby does have a few surprising modifications under the hood." He patted the van. "Anyway, did the trick."

She hugged him. "Thanks, Oshiro."

"No problem. June said she'd bug out with you guys anytime—between Nick and Megan, she got more rest and quiet time than she has in months."

Megan was scrutinizing the empty parking lot. "Mom, where's your car? How are we getting home?"

Lucy cringed, knowing she'd have to explain about the bomb sooner or later. Knowing Megan, she would get over the fact that her mother was almost killed faster than she'd forgive them for not telling her right away.

"We can go home, right?" Nick said. "It's safe."

"It's safe, just not so private. The techs are still removing all the bugs from the house and your car." Thankfully, Valencia was picking up the tab for the cleanup and letting Lucy use one of her vehicles in the meantime.

"So what really happened?" Megan bounced up the steps leading to the front door as the adults followed more slowly. "We heard the news about Marcus Gold's party, but you always have the inside scoop."

They gathered in the workroom of Lucy's team, since it was Sunday and no one else was there. She gave them a brief rundown of the events of the night before, though sanitized for Megan's ears.

"Graham Hunt and Marcus Gold." Oshiro rolled their names as if they had a bad taste. "How many people's lives were destroyed because of their frat-boy feud?"

"Graham told me Marcus was a charismatic psychopath. He just never bothered to mention that he was one as well."

"The news said Graham was shot and killed," Nick said, "and only that Marcus was hospitalized. Is he under arrest? Is he going to blame you and come after us again? I mean, the man burned down his own mother's house and kidnapped you." His gaze fell on Megan. Lucy understood his real question. Is our family safe?

"Gold was overdosed with the same drug he used to facilitate his assaults. The doctors say he doesn't remember anything."

"Anything about last night?" Oshiro asked. "Or anything about his crimes so he'll get off on a diminished-capacity plea?" It was clear he was skeptical about the billionaire's amnesia. Lucy would have been as well if she hadn't seen Judi Miller and the catastrophic results of the drug firsthand. And if anyone knew the dosage required to create those results, it would have been Tandi Jefferson.

"Can't remember his life. Not after the age of eight. It was a massive overdose, and apparently Tandi Jefferson tweaked it to be even more potent. The doctors aren't sure if the effects are permanent, but the other victim who survived a similar overdose has shown no recovery in two years."

"A brilliant mind, erased in a second," Nick mused.

"This is why you say no to drugs," Megan put in, her tone that of a TV commercial announcer. Everyone chuckled. "So unless Marcus Gold is faking it—and if he is, and he tries anything, then the police will know he's faking it, and he'll go to jail—then you're safe? He won't come after you again, right?"

Lucy smiled at how her daughter, in one breath no less, encapsulated the heart of the argument. "Right. I don't see any way Gold could target us without putting himself behind bars."

Nick obviously wasn't as certain. "Man's a billionaire, resources around the world, a ton of political influence, and a sociopath who enjoys holding a grudge. What if this amnesia wears off? Just enough for him to get word out to his gang of goons to send them after you?"

"Then I'll bring them down like I brought down Hunt and Gold," Lucy answered. Megan grinned, but Lucy knew Nick saw through her false bravado. After all, she hadn't really brought down Gold—that was Tandi Jefferson. Maybe they could have built a strong enough case, given time and the cooperation of Rebekah Hunt, but with Graham's death, even that was uncertain.

"So the only two people paying for these crimes are one of the victims and the wife?" Oshiro asked, changing the subject after the silence grew uncomfortable. "I'd much rather it was Hunt and Gold rotting away behind bars."

"Rebekah is already pleading diminished capacity—says Hunt forced her to help him, and if she hadn't agreed, he would have killed Alina. Said she was a victim as well, in constant terror for her life." Lucy didn't bother to hide her disdain for that particular legal maneuver.

"But wait," Megan said. "Why did Alina kill herself? What about the baby?"

"Cassandra Hart—she's our client—was Alina's doctor. She says Rebekah drove Alina to kill herself. Literally took her to the bridge, made her strip naked so there'd be no evidence of where she'd been held, and told her if she didn't jump, Hunt would kill the baby."

They were all silent for a long moment.

"She was how old?" Nick asked.

"Just turned nineteen."

"Wow," Megan said. "She loved her baby that much. She's the real hero. Alina."

Lucy nodded. "Without her, we might never have discovered Hunt and Gold's sadistic game. Who knows how many victims there might have been?"

"And you know they would have escalated to killing them," Nick said.

"So where's the baby?" Oshiro asked.

Lucy brightened. "That's the one piece of good news to come out of all this. Megan, you have a new babysitting client if you want. Dr. Hart and Detective Drake are adopting Alina's baby."

Valencia rushed in, appearing more flustered than Lucy had ever seen her before.

"What's wrong? Did they find something at our house?" Lucy asked, avoiding the word bomb for Megan's sake.

"No. It's TK. With everything happening here yesterday and last night, I didn't even notice. I should have noticed, she promised, and she always keeps her promises—" Valencia blew her breath out and sank into a chair, suddenly appearing older than her sixty-some years. "She never checked in. She's not answering her phone. I can't reach her."

"She took one of your cars, right? Have you

checked its location?" Lucy asked, cursing herself—her phone had been in the custody of Gold's people and then turned off, so she had no idea if TK had tried to contact her. Or had asked for help, only to receive silence.

"That's what's so worrisome," Valencia answered. "TK said she was going to Alabama to see her friend from the Marines. According to the GPS, she made it to Oneonta. But then last night she drove to northern Georgia. And that's where the car still is."

"If you know where she is, why are you so worried?" Megan asked. "I mean, cell phones die or sometimes don't have many bars." Her own two favorite excuses for not checking in when she was meant to. But Megan was a teenager—TK knew better. Although she had seemed preoccupied, concerned about her friend. Lucy realized she didn't even know the name of that friend.

"That's why I'm so worried," Valencia said. "I pulled up the satellite view of where the car is. It's in the middle of a forest. Nothing around for miles and miles." She looked up at Lucy. "I know you've been through a lot these past few days." She included Nick and Megan in her glance. "All of you. But—"

"TK is family," Nick answered for Lucy.

Oshiro made a huffing noise. "And you just happen to have the best tracker on the East Coast sitting right here."

"I can't ask you," Lucy said. "June and the baby—"

"Can come stay with us," Nick said. "Let us

return the hospitality."

"Are you sure?" Lucy asked Nick, ignoring the others. She knew they still had a conversation to have, after the target Gold had put on her family. She had no idea how she'd answer his concerns, especially now that she no longer had the FBI to shield and protect them, but she didn't want him to feel as if she was taking advantage of TK's disappearance to avoid him.

He lay his hand on top of hers and squeezed. "Go. Bring TK home. We'll be here."

Lucy pushed back her chair, and Oshiro followed. "Valencia, show us where you found the car. And let's call in Wash, see if there's any data from her cell phone that might help."

"Who's the Marine she went to see?" Oshiro asked.

"I don't know, but that's number one on my list of questions." She paused to give both Nick and Megan quick hugs. "I'll see you guys soon."

"Go find TK, Mom," Megan said. "But be careful."

"Always."

About CJ:

New York Times and *USA Today* bestselling author of over forty novels, former pediatric ER doctor CJ Lyons has lived the life she writes about in her cutting-edge Thrillers with Heart.

Two-time winner of the International Thriller Writers' coveted Thriller Award, CJ has been called a "master within the genre" (Pittsburgh Magazine) and her work has been praised as "breathtakingly fast-paced" and "riveting" (Publishers Weekly) with "characters with beating hearts and three dimensions" (Newsday).

Learn more about CJ's Thrillers with Heart at www.CJLyons.net

www.ingramcontent.com/pod-product-compliance
Lightning Source LLC
Chambersburg PA
CBHW061621190726
48288CB00007B/2416